CONNECTED TO THE PLUG

DWAN MARQUIS WILLIAMS

Good2Go Publishing

Connected To The Plug
Written by Dwan Marquis Williams
Cover Design: Davida Baldwin
Typesetter: Mychea
ISBN: 978-1-943686-37-7
Copyright ©2017 Good2Go Publishing
Published 2017 by Good2Go Publishing
7311 W. Glass Lane • Laveen, AZ 85339
www.good2gopublishing.com
https://twitter.com/good2gobooks
G2G@good2gopublishing.com
www.facebook.com/good2gopublishing
www.instagram.com/good2gopublishing

Acknowledgments

Jamarielle "K.B." Darden,

Jasper Allen, S. Harper and K Floyed

CONNECTED TO THE PLUG

Prologue

"Yo, don't have me out there waiting on your stupid ass all day neither," Menace barked at the caller on the other end of the phone.

"Come on, dawg, don't even try to play me like that," J.B. laughed before Menace hung up the phone in his ear. Menace hated serving J.B. Mainly because J.B. lived on the north side of town, where he had major beef with a couple of guys and he knew if he got caught slipping on their turf it would be his ass.

After Menace weighed out the four and a half ounces that J.B. ordered, he checked his clip, tucked his nina in his waistline, and then headed down the stairs to the front door. "Aye, Ma. If anybody call or come by looking for me, tell 'em I'll be back in about an hour," Menace told his mother, Ms. Louise as he retrieved his jacket from the coat rack beside the front door.

"Where you going?" Ms. Louis asked, never taking her eyes from the television set. Little Tommy sat up with a big smile on his face as he listened to the conversation between his mother and big brother.

"I'm about to go to the store," Menace lied once he had his jacket on. That was all Tommy needed to hear.

"I wanna go," Little Tommy screamed, always jumping at the opportunity to hang with his older brother.

Little Tommy was a thirteen-year-old version of his big brother, Menace. Tall, lanky, gray eyes, curly hair, and all. He worshiped the ground his brother walked on and wanted to be just like him when he grew up. Menace loved his brother just as much and showed it by spoiling him to no end so he wouldn't resort to the streets as Menace had coming up. Whatever Tommy wanted, all he had to do was let his big brother know, and that's exactly what he did.

Menace paused for a second as Tommy ran out of the living room and snatched his coat off the coat rack. He stared at Menace with hopeful eyes as he slid into it, waiting for him to say that it was okay, but before he could say anything, Ms. Louis spoke up. "Go ahead and spend some quality time with your little brother before you hit them streets." Menace looked Tommy in the eyes and then took off his hat and placed it on Tommy's tiny head. He laughed to himself as the brim of the hat covered Tommy's head and hung slightly above his eyes. Little Tommy smiled as Menace put his hand on top of Tommy's head and told him to come on.

"As soon as I make this run, I'ma take you to the mall and buy you an outfit and a new pair of Js for making the honor roll," Menace promised Little Tommy as he started the engine to his brand-new Benz and pulled from the curb.

"Yo, this ride is hot," Tommy admitted as he stuck his arm out the window. "When I grow up I wanna be just like you, Menace." Menace took his eyes off of the road for a second and glanced over at his little brother as Tommy stared out the window at a group of girls dressed in Daisy Dukes and halter tops. Trying to beat the heat. Tommy felt like "the man" as the young girls smiled and waved at them as they passed by.

"Nah, lil bruh," Menace replied getting Tommy's attention. "You gonna be better than I am. That's why I push you so hard and reward you for doing well in school. If you don't remember anything else I have taught you, I want you to remember this:"—Tommy saw the seriousness in Menaces eyes as he paid close attention— "Education comes first." Little Tommy took in the jewel Menace had just dropped on him and nodded his head in understanding. "Then you get the money and bitches," Menace joked, bringing a smiled back to Little Tommy's face. That's what he liked about Menace. Although he was serious, he would bring back the fun in every situation.

***

"Yo, where you at?" Menace yelled into his phone at J.B. Menace had been sitting in front of Finch Street Park for over ten minutes now waiting on him to show. He instantly regretted not having J.B come to his side of town. He felt like a sitting duck waiting to be killed.

"I'm right around the corner. I'll be there in less

than one minute," J.B. claimed as Menace ended the call frustrated and then checked his surroundings for anything out of the ordinary. Two minutes later, Menace noticed J.B.'s old Toyota Corolla come smoking around the corner. As much money as J.B. should have been making, Menace couldn't understand for the life of him why he wouldn't invest a couple grand into a new whip. "Sit tight. I'll be right back," Menace told little Tommy as he got out of his car to meet J.B. in the park. The park was rather empty for a Saturday evening. That was good with Menace. That meant there wouldn't be many eyes in his business, and that he could keep his eyes open for anyone that looked suspicious.

"My fault, homie. I had to drop my baby mama off at the beauty salon," J.B. apologized as he went into his pocket to pull out money for the pack. After making sure all $3,200 was there, Menace went into one of his cargo pants pockets and pulled out a big ziplock bag filled with work. Menace watched J.B. get into his car and pull off before he made his way to his car. As soon as he reached for the door handle, a strange feeling came over him that made him glance at the corner. There he noticed a dark blue four door hooptie creeping his way. Just as he put his hand on his 9mm, bullets began to ring out. Menace quickly jumped over the hood of his Benz, took cover, and then returned fire. The small shootout only lasted a few seconds, but to the few pedestrians at the park, it seemed to last a lifetime as they scattered for shelter from the rapid gunfire from Menace's loud cannon and the semi-automatic weapons from the hooptie.

Once the shots ceased, Menace stood to his feet and looked around into the park. He saw a little girl, no older than six years old, laid out in the middle of the merry-go-round, in a puddle of her own blood. "Damn," he cursed to himself as he turned to check on Little Tommy. When he opened the passenger's side door all he could do was stare in disbelief as his only brother took his last breath and closed his teary eyes.

1

"*Yo, Tawana?*" *Speedy called* out from their bedroom.

"I'm about to be out," she replied.

He sat at the foot of the bed and slid his feet into the brand-new pair of Timberland boots he bought the day before.

"Now that's what I'm talking about," he said, looking at his feet before he threw on his forty inch Cuban-linked chain.

The red diamond-encrusted boxing glove charm that hung from it brought out the word Polo written in red on his gray Polo jogging suit.

Speedy was a slim, dark-skinned cat with what most people referred to as sneaky eyes, which stayed half-way shut, due to his constant weed habit that he obtained when he was coming up. He was well-known and respected throughout the city for his many brawls and countless shoot-outs over the years.

The name Speedy was given to him one day when he and a local stick-up kid, who went by the name of Trigga, got into a heated argument that ended with Trigga pulling out a .38 Special on him. Trigga had it cocked back and aimed at the center of Speedy's forehead, but before he could pull the trigger, Speedy caught him with a quick two-piece that knocked him out cold. Another reason people called him Speedy was because he talked a hundred miles per hour at all times.

"I'm going to need some money for gas and food before you leave, Marcus," his girlfriend, Tawana, shouted out from the bathroom as she jumped out of the shower.

She smiled to herself while putting on a model pose, admiring her voluptuous-sized breasts and shapely hips in the full-length mirror that hung behind the bathroom door. She then wrapped herself up in a Sean John towel when she was done. No matter where she went, with or without her better half, she gained the attention of both men and women the same. She was often called the "Black Beauty" by guys while growing up in her old north side neighborhood.

Tawana was in her senior year when she first caught Speedy's eyes. She was walking home from school one day in a pair of blue Baby Phat jeans that looked as if they were painted on her, with her belly button showing from the matching halter top. Her blue and white Air Max made it seem as if she was walking on air as she approached the corner store.

"Yo! What's up which ya, lil mama?" Speedy called out as she strolled passed the group of young hustlers shooting a game of C-low in front of the store.

She rolled her eyes and kept on walking like she didn't hear him, but little did she know, he was very persistent.

"What's the password?" he asked as he jumped in front of her to block her from entering the store.

He smiled, revealing a mouth full of gold fronts and a dimple in his left cheek. She couldn't front, Speedy was a guy she knew she could fall for, but at the time, the only thing on her mind was getting some nicotine into her system. Without giving him any further thought, Tawana walked around him and made her way into the store.

"Damn, bruh," Menace clowned his friend, who then got off his knees and stood to his feet. He held the three dice in his left hand while shaking them. "She just played the shit out of you, homie."

Menace then bent back down and released the dice from his hand as the other bystanders agreed. Tawana heard Menace's statement right before the door closed behind her, and smiled.

Speedy looked at his friend and huffed. "Nigga, please! I bet y'all I come back out with her number," Speedy bet as he popped his collar and then pulled out a $100 bill and threw it to the ground. "Yeah, that's what I thought," he bragged.

He looked at each one of the hustlers in their faces to see who would take the bet. Always in competition with each other, Menace pulled off a $100 bill from the money he had in his hand and covered it like it was nothing.

4

"I'll take that gentleman's bet, my nigga. You must think you's me or somebody," Menace joked as he gave a pound to the guy beside him who was watching the game.

Before he could roll the dice again, two more bystanders placed a $100 bill down to make their bets as well. Once Speedy covered everyone's bet, he made his way into the store to complete his mission.

"C-low, muthafuckas," Menace screamed just as Speedy entered the store.

As soon as the door closed behind him, Speedy's eyes began to roam the store in search of his prey. It didn't take long for him to find her at the counter waiting for the store owner, Arab Mike, to get the footstool from the corner so he could grab a pack of Newports from the top shelf.

After retrieving them, Mike came down, placed them on the counter top in front of her, and said, "That'll be $3.75."

Tawana dug into her handbag to get the money out.

"I'm also going to need to see your ID," Mike told her, looking   at her suspiciously.

Tawana rolled her eyes and dug a bit deeper. She bypassed her ID card as she tried to think of a lie to shoot to him since she was only seventeen years old.

˄ "Ohhmmm, I must have left it in my other handbag, sir," she replied as she then looked into his eyes.

She couldn't believe Mike was trying to card her, since she came to his store at least twice a week to buy her pack of cancer sticks. The stare-down between the two lasted a few seconds before Mike finally spoke up.

"Well," he began as he leaned over the countertop toward her.

She could tell by the way he smiled at her that she had him under her spell like she had the rest of the guys who had the pleasure of being in her presence.

"No ID, no cigarettes, pretty!" Mike calmly stated as he looked her in her face.

Tawana narrowed her eyes into small slits and

took a deep breath as she fumed inside. Right when she creased her lips to give him a tongue lashing of a lifetime, Speedy intervened.

"I got 'em, Mike."

Speedy walked up to the counter beside her and pulled out a bank roll of bills. He found a $20 bill and then handed it to Mike.

"Keep the change," Speedy told him as he looked in Tawana's direction.

Not at all impressed, Tawana sucked her teeth, snatched the Newports off the countertop, and then marched out of the store.

"Damn, lil mama!" Speedy called out to Tawana as she headed up the street. "You at least could've said thank you for the favor I just did for you."

After letting out a huge cloud of smoke, she spun around on her heels to address him. Speedy swallowed the lump that had formed in his throat as she made her way back over in his direction. He tried to play it cool, but deep down inside he was more nervous than a hooker in church on a Sunday morning. After running game for several minutes,

7

Tawana finally folded and agreed to let him take her out on a date.

Ever since that day, the two had been inseparable. That was a little over five years ago.

"Yo, don't call me Marcus," Speedy warned heatedly.

"Whatever, Mar-cuuus," Tawana repeated, followed by a slight giggle.

She knew calling Speedy by his government name would get him uptight, but she did it anyway just to see the way he flared his nostrils when he got mad.

"One, two, three!" Tawana counted as Speedy stormed through the bathroom door.

His screw face softened once she dropped the towel from around her body to reveal her nakedness to him. No matter how many times he'd seen her body, it always seemed to amaze him. He stood frozen like a deer stuck in headlights as her deep brown nipples put him in a trance.

"What's the matter, Mar-cuuus? Cat got your tongue now?" she teased before she walked over to him and placed a finger under his chin to close his mouth.

She placed her lips on his and a slight moan escaped her as he slid his tongue into her mouth. He gripped both of her ass cheeks and then grinded his midsection into hers, and she instantly became moist.

"Uh, uh!" she protested, and took a step back to regain her composure. "You are not about to make me late for school again, boy. If you wanted to get a quickie, you should've joined me in the shower."

Speedy stared at her lustfully as he massaged his rock-hard erection.

"Come on, Tawana," he pouted like a kid, giving her his best sad face.

After seeing the look she was giving him, Speedy knew there was no need to try to persuade her any further.

"Yeah, yeah, yeah! How much you need?" he asked as he then pulled out a wad of money.

He flipped through several bills until Tawana snatched the wad out of his hand, leaving him with the five twenties he had pulled off for her.

"This will do," she replied as she walked around him and into their bedroom.

Speedy shook his head from side to side as he watched Tawana's ass cheeks bounce with each step she took as he followed close behind her. She walked over to the dresser, grabbed a bottle of lotion, and then began to apply some onto her beautiful, toned legs. That was his cue. Speedy snuck up behind her, slapped her ass as hard as he could, and then jumped back and watched it jiggle.

"Ouch!" Tawana screamed as she stood straight up and turned around.

Speedy saw the fire in her eyes and started backpedaling toward the bedroom door to the hallway. As soon as he touched the door knob, Tawana rushed him with cat-like speed, throwing punches wildly.

Ducking and dodging, Speedy escaped without a single blow being landed. Once he made it into the hallway, he quickly slammed the door, separating them from each other before jetting toward the front door. By the time he reached the front door, he turned around and saw Tawana's naked body running in his direction with her quickness.

"And get your hair done while you're out," he joked as he slammed the front door behind him before she could get to him.

By the time he got to his car, Tawana had opened the door and stuck her head out.

"You wasn't saying that last night when I had those toes curled up like the Wicked Witch of the West," she laughed as she put up her middle finger and then flicked her tongue out at him.

He knew she was telling the truth because her head game was on 110. Speedy shook his head as he put his key in the ignition, started the engine, and threw up the deuces before pulling off. Tawana smiled as she closed the front door shut and then hurried back into their room so she could get dressed. She was determined not to be late again for fooling around with Speedy.

2

Speedy nodded his head in approval as he pulled up in front of the spot and watched his partner, Menace, run game on a bad-ass, redboned chick from around the neighborhood.

Speedy didn't know her name, but he had seen her out and about plenty of times before.

Menace and Speedy had been best friends since grade school. Throughout the years they had made a name for themselves in the streets for getting money and hos—not to mention for busting a head or two along the way. Menace stood about six foot tall, and he had light skin with an athletic build. His good hair gained the attention from females wherever he went. That alone started a lot of the beef with rival hood crews around the city.

"What's up, shorty?" Speedy asked the redbone as she passed him on her way out of the fence that surrounded the spot.

She smiled and then waved her hand as she popped her bubblegum, all while never breaking her stride.

"Damn! She got a phat ass," Speedy admitted as he walked up and stood beside Menace.

They both stared at her viciously until she was out of sight.

"Yo! You bring the blunts?" Menace asked as he dug inside his North Face jacket and pulled out a ziplock bag full of "PURP."

Speedy went into his pants pocket and flashed a four pack of White Owl cigars, which he then waved in the air.

"And you know this, mannn," Speedy replied, sounding like Smokey from the movie *Friday*.

They then walked up to the porch and took a seat on the steps as Menace took one of the cigars and emptied its contents onto the ground beside him. Once it was empty, he filled it to capacity with the potent weed. As soon as he   finished rolling up and was about to light it, Shelia came out of the spot and stood between them.

Shelia's house was known around the way as "the spot." Not only was it where they hung out, but it was also where they trapped. Shelia was much older than the two, and although she was now only a bag of bones, she was one of the baddest females walking the streets of Wilson when she was in her prime. She turned Speedy and Menace on to the game a few years back when her ex-boyfriend got caught up in a conspiracy by the feds. They had been climbing up the ladder of success since then.

"Let me hit that?" Shelia asked, inching closer.

"I got what you want, auntie," Menace replied as he then dug deep into his pocket and pulled out a see-through vial of crack.

Her eyes lit up instantly as she watched the fish scale of the rocks glisten in the sunlight. She quickly grabbed the vial out of his hand as if it would disappear at any moment. After tucking it in her bosom, she tightened her loose-fitting robe back around her body.

"Auntie, you need to get off that shit. I remember when you used to have every nigga in the neighborhood chasing after you."

Shelia smiled as she took a short trip down memory lane to her heyday, back when she could have had any hustler or white-collar man she desired. Those thoughts were short-lived when she thought about the good feeling she would be feeling once she met up with "Scotty" when she put her crack on the stem she had waiting on her in her bedroom.

"I'ma quit real soon, nephew," she promised as she began to backpedal toward the front door in an attempt to make her exit.

Speedy and Menace looked at each other, and then back at Shelia before smacking their lips. They had heard that promise many times before, and they were not sold on it.

"I'm for real. Y'all will see. Just watch."

She disappeared into the spot, slamming the door behind her, and rushed to get her early-morning fix. They could hear her taking two steps at a time as she raced upstairs to get beamed up.

Speedy and Menace had really tried to get Shelia

off drugs in the past. They went as far as sending her to a rehab center in Goldsboro, North Carolina, which was short-lived because she was back at the spot within a week doing her thing once again. After finding out she was HIV positive, Speedy and Menace began giving her free crack, reasoning that they would rather give it to her instead of letting her go out and steal, beg, or borrow to get it—or even worse, sell her body and infect someone else to get high.

It was a little past noon, and they were halfway finished with the work they had brought out with them when they looked up and noticed an old raggedy blue and gray Chevy pickup truck pull up in front of the spot. Smoke clouded the truck and it backfired before it was turned off.

"I got this one," Menace said as he passed the blunt to his partner and stood to his feet. "What you need?" he asked the slim, white crackhead once he stepped out of the truck and made his way to the fence entrance.

"I need a fifty," the crackhead answered,

reaching into his shirt pocket to pull out a crisp $50 bill.

Menace took the bill and held it in the air to make sure it was real. After he was satisfied, he wrapped it around the other bills he had collected that day, and then put the wad back in his pocket.

"You ain't the police or nothing, are you?" Menace asked as he pulled out three vials of crack that he juggled in his hand.

"The police?" the crackhead questioned. "Do I look like a pig to you?"

Menace looked at the crackhead's dry and chapped lips. The way he scratched at his arms through the thin fabric of his worn shirt indicated a true junkie's itch. And when he looked up and down the block like he was paranoid, Menace knew he was the real deal. Menace handed over the drugs that the fiend paid for, and he then took a step back.

"Let's hope for your sake that you're not the police," Menace threatened as he held out his right arm and formed his fingers as if they were a gun. Menace then pulled the imaginary trigger.

"BANG," he whispered as if he'd just hit his mark.

The crackhead ignored the gesture, headed toward his truck, and then jumped in. He made three attempts at starting it before it backfired twice and came to life. A cloud of smoke formed around it before the truck puttered down the block, killing every mosquito in sight.

LATER THAT NIGHT

"So, what you gettin' into tonight?" Menace asked as they sat in the spot and counted up all the money they made for the day. Speedy sat across the table from his partner with a blunt hanging from his lips, in deep concentration.

"I don't know for real. I was thinking about heading to The Twilight Zone later on. Why, what you trying to do?" Speedy asked as he stopped counting to look up at Menace.

"Shit. I'm trying to hit the club up wit' you."

Speedy nodded his head in agreement as he took another pull from the blunt. He exhaled the smoke

Overdue fines are 25¢ per day and the maximum
fine per item is $10.00.
****

Title:	Street rap /
Item ID:	871091006478179
Due:	05/05/2022

Title:	Connected to the plug /
Item ID:	871091006155730
Due:	05/05/2022

Title:
Thin line between death and dishonor /
Item ID:	871091006199676
Due:	05/05/2022

Title:	A hustler's son :
Item ID:	871091005977995
Due:	04/28/2022

Title:	Stand by your truth :
Item ID:	871091006227899
Due:	04/28/2022

into the air and almost choked from laughing.

"What's so funny, my nigga?" Menace asked as he put a rubber band around the last stack of bills.

"You sure your mama gonna let you hang out wit' your homie tonight?" Speedy joked, referring to Menace's girlfriend, Crystal.

Menace had to join in on the joke and admit that Crystal was nothing to play with. She had proven that on plenty of occasions by jumping on him after she finished beating the living daylights out of a bitch for being all up in her man's face. She also proved how down she was when she helped Speedy and Menace set up a few niggas when they were on the come-up. Her sweet and innocent school-girl look fooled a lot of her victims. Crystal's sister, Tawana, introduced them to one another shortly after she and Speedy began dating, and they hadn't looked back since.

"What? I know you ain't talking, because unlike you, I really do wear the pants up in my house," Menace boasted before he snatched the dangling blunt out of Speedy's mouth and took a long pull.

Speedy looked at his partner with doubt clearly written all over his face. "Well I guess the man has spoken then." Speedy stood to his feet and prepared to leave. "I'll be over to get you around midnight."

Menace threw up the peace sign as Speedy turned toward the door. Before walking out, he placed two vials filled with crack rocks on the coffee table for Sheila. He then closed the door behind him, leaving Menace to clean up the mess they had made throughout the day.

* * *

As soon as Speedy entered the house, he was met by the aroma of Tawana's cucumber melon body spray. He smiled, closed the front door behind him, and then made his way to the bedroom where he knew she was waiting for him. He smiled when he reached the bedroom door and peeked in. There she was lying on her back with her legs spread wide open, playing with herself.

"It's about time," she announced in a low and seductive tone while rubbing her pointer and index fingers in a circular motion over her swollen clit.

Her eyes closed as her mouth fell open and her body began to shake uncontrollably. Speedy's manhood instantly grew to its full length in no time. He massaged himself and watched her bring pleasure to herself. Just the sight of her juices flowing from her vagina almost made him cum all over himself.

"Come and get it, daddy," Tawana begged as she placed both of her legs into the air.

Speedy made his way to the foot of their bed and took off all of his clothes. He watched her finger disappear and then reappear from her tunnel of love.

Not being able to take anymore, Speedy plunged his face into her pool of wetness and sent her straight to ecstasy.

"Right there, baby," she coached as she guided the back of his head to her spot and held it there.

The more he licked, the harder she grinded his tongue.

"I'm cumming," she screamed as she tried to get out of his grasp.

She began to cum even harder once Speedy slid

his thumb in her ass.

"Shit!" she cried out, and then placed her palms on his forehead and tried to push his face away but it was no use.

She slid so far back, she found herself pinned to the headboard.

"Look whose toes are curling up like the Wicked Witch of the West now," Speedy bragged once he let her go.

He hovered over her as her body jerked in the middle of the bed. He knew she was spent as she gazed at the ceiling fan going round and round. Before Tawana even had a chance to respond, Speedy roughly grabbed her by her waist, flipped her onto her stomach, and then entered her from behind. They went at it like wild animals.

"Beat this pussy, daddy," Tawana begged as she arched her back and met him pound for pound.

"Whose pussy is this?" he asked as he slapped her backside several times, leaving his handprint with each hit.

"Yours, daddy," she replied, never breaking

stride.

She bit down on her bottom lip and then turned her head to look back at him.

"I'm cumming, baby!" she warned as she reached between her legs and played with her clit.

Speedy looked down and watched as he went in and out of her with precision. When Tawana came, her body went limp under his, and they collapsed on the bed together. Once Speedy gained enough strength, he got up and looked at Tawana as cum oozed out of her pussy. He then made his way to the bathroom.

Thirty minutes later, Speedy reentered the bedroom dripping wet with a towel wrapped around the lower half of his body, exposing his bare chest.

"Where are you about to go?" Tawana asked as she watched him walk across the room into the walk-in closet.

She placed a pillow between her legs to stop the tingling sensation that began to grow. She put her thumb in her mouth to control her craving as she waited for him to respond.

"Menace and I are about to go out to The Twilight Zone," he replied nonchalantly as he began to get dressed.

Tawana removed her thumb from her mouth to suck her teeth. Speedy knew she was going to pitch a fit, but he gave his friend his word he was going out—and he intended to keep it.

"Why you going out, baby?" she asked sweetly as she batted her eyes. "Why don't you come back to bed and cuddle up with me tonight?"

Tawana poked out her bottom lip and let out a deep sigh. She knew the look she was giving him always worked, but her belief slowly started fading when he continued to get dressed.

"Because I told him I would go out with him," Speedy replied once he was fully dressed.

He then looked into the mirror to check out his gear, and made sure everything was intact. Tawana had to admit Speedy was looking good in his all-black Red Label True Religion outfit with a pair of True Religion tennis shoes. She knew at that point there was no need to keep trying to talk him into staying home, so she just rolled her eyes, turned her back to him, and then threw the comforter over her head. Speedy began to feel guilty when he saw the covers slowly move up and down as Tawana took breath after breath.

"Come on, Tawana," he pleaded once he slid his chain over his head.

"Just go ahead and leave, Marcus, before we start arguing," she protested as she heard his footsteps nearing the bed.

A second later she felt the weight of Speedy's body on top of her, and he began to tickle her frantically.

"Stop, boy!" she laughed while trying to get him off.

"You mad at me?" he asked while continuing his torture.

She squirmed but couldn't get herself free.

"No, no, no!" she lied, hoping he would show mercy.

"You lying," he accused as he kept on with his plan.

He knew that if he tickled her long enough, she would eventually pee on herself, and that's what he intended on doing.

"Stop, Speedy! You're gonna make me pee on myself, boy," she warned as tears formed in the corners of her eyes.

He smiled on the inside at how his plan was coming together perfectly. "Oh well."

Within a minute's time, Tawana became serious as her bladder gave way. Speedy quickly hopped to his feet as Tawana got strength from out of nowhere and knocked him off the top of her. He gathered his footing, and Tawana stumbled to the bedroom door.

"I'ma get yo' ass, Marcus!" Tawana threatened as she hopped her naked ass out of bed and stomped in his direction with her fists balled into knots. "Ewwww, I hate you so much!" she screamed at the top of her lungs and then began to throw haymakers at him.

Speedy dodged them all with ease, laughing the entire time.

"I love you too," he joked as he grabbed Tawana

and then shoved her backward.

He slammed the door between them and took off down the hall toward the front door. By the time Tawana opened the door to their bedroom, she heard the front door slam shut. She cursed out Speedy, turned around, and headed to the bathroom to clean herself up, vowing to get him back.

3

"Speedy, here!" Crystal called out to Menace as she led him into the living room. "You want something to drink?" she offered as she made her way into the kitchen to fix herself a cup of Kool-Aid.

"Nah, I'm good, lil sis!" he replied as he sat down on the sofa and made himself comfortable.

He grabbed the remote from the coffee table and flipped through the channels until he found the station for which he was looking.

"Turn that up!" Crystal screamed before she danced her way back into the front room. "That's my shit right there!"

She joyfully sang the lyrics to the song "Right Thurr" by Chingy as she shook what her mamma gave her. By the time the video went off, she was completely out of breath.

"Whew! That was like a workout in itself," Crystal joked as she then took a seat next to Speedy.

"Where my sister at, big bruh?" she asked once she caught her breath.

"She should be just getting out of the shower by now," he claimed with a big smile on his face.

Crystal eyed him suspiciously, knowing he wasn't being completely honest with her.

"Uh huh! I'ma call her and see what you done did to my sister."

Unable to hold in his laugh any longer, he let it out and Crystal did the same. She knew they always stayed into something and sometimes wished that she and Menace had the kind of relationship her sister and Speedy shared.

"Why you always accusing me of doing something to her? Why can't she be the one doing something to me?" he asked, looking like an innocent school boy.

Crystal scrunched up her lips. But before she had the chance to respond, Menace appeared from the back room.

"You ready, my dude?"

Crystal and Speedy both looked up in the

doorway to check him out. He stood there with a cocky smile on his face and spread his arms out so they could get a clear view.

"Y'all like?" he asked as he did a 360 to show off his denim blue Akademic outfit with a crisp new pair of white Air Force Ones on his feet.

"Saved by the bell," Speedy thought to himself as he stood to his feet and gave his partner some dap.

After their short embrace, Crystal rolled her eyes and then cleared her throat. "Anyways! Menace, don't let the sun beat yo' ass home," Crystal threatened with one hand on her hip as she stared him up and down.

"And you said you wear the pants in your house," Speedy laughed under his breath and shot his partner a look.

"Yeah, yeah, yeah!" Menace replied as he took off in the direction of the front door.

He didn't feel like getting into it with Crystal at the time, so he just ignored her little demand, but she was dead on his trail.

"Yo! Let me holla at her for a second," Menace

told his partner as he opened the front door.

Speedy smiled as he walked out the door, knowing the drill too well.

A couple of minutes passed before Menace headed out the door and to the car.

Before they pulled off, Crystal yelled out from the doorway. "Oh yeah! Don't think I ain't gonna call Tawana to see what you did to her," she assured Speedy.

He laughed at her comment and thought back to Tawana's naked body running toward him at full speed as he closed the door behind him. He turned up his system, blew the horn, and stepped on the gas as they headed to the club.

* * *

As soon as they entered The Twilight Zone, they were greeted by small-time corner hustlers, major figures in the game, and hood rats from every neighborhood in the city that were trying to get chosen for the night. They acknowledged each and every one of them with daps and short embraces, firm handshakes, or nods of their heads, before they made their way to their favorite area, the bar, without breaking a single stride.

"Let's get two bottles of Moët," Speedy ordered as he dug into his pocket and pulled out a bankroll of money.

The barmaid's eyes beamed in on the bills, and the thought of the big tip she knew she would receive flashed through her mind instantly.

"That will be $300," she informed Speedy as she eyed him seductively and then licked her lips.

Speedy smiled as he handed her four $100 bills.

"Keep the change," he said as he slid the money into her hands.

She blushed, turned around, and headed to the cooler in the back where they kept all the champagne. Speedy was thinking about the many positions he could put her in after the club, when his thoughts were disturbed by two attractive females laughing out loud. He and Menace turned around just as one started to order.

"Can I have two glasses of Moscato?" the short, thick, and light-complexioned female asked.

Once the bartender told her the price, she went into her oversized Christian Dior handbag to get her wallet out, but before she could pay for it, Menace intervened.

"Make that a bottle of Moscato for the prettiest ladies in the place," he complimented while staring at the brown-skinned beauty in front of him.

"One bottle coming up," the bartender announced as he turned to walk away.

Menace chuckled and then stopped the bartender before he could make his exit.

"No, you must have misunderstood me, my man."

The bartender stood with a confused expression on his face.

"I meant a bottle for each one of the ladies," Menace clarified while pulling out a wad of money and removing two $100 bills to take care of the order.

Menace peeped how the brown-skinned female's eyes lit up before he put the wad back into his pocket. Just as her light-complexioned friend was about to protest, the brown-skinned woman spoke up before she could: "Thank you very much, handsome."

She held out her hand for Menace to shake, which he did. He then asked for her name.

"My name is Tammie, but my friends call me Red for short," she replied shyly as she found herself lost in Menace's deep gray eyes.

He nodded his head in approval as he admired the way Red's Dior Jeans hugged each and every one of her many curves. What really caught his attention were the six-inch Dior heels she wore that complimented her natural reddish-brown-colored hair.

"So, can I be one of those friends who calls you Red?" Menace flirted as he licked his lips.

"I think we might be able to make that possible," she flirted back.

He could tell she was really feeling his swagger by the way he had her smiling from ear to ear. They stood quietly staring into each other's eyes with dirty thoughts running through their minds, before the light-skinned woman spoke up and broke their trains of thought.

"Anyways!" she said as she turned in Speedy's direction to address him. "My name is Chantel, but my friends call me Fuzzy," she mimicked her friend.

Chantel held out her hand to Speedy. He readily accepted it and then planted a soft kiss on the back side of it.

"My friend can be so rude at times," Chantel said as she glanced over at Red, who, in return, hunched her shoulders and turned her attention back to Menace.

"Nice to meet you. My friends all call me Speedy," he replied as he cleared his throat and then looked into her eyes.

He fell into a trance at her beauty. As a matter of fact, no other woman besides Tawana had ever captured his undivided attention the way she was doing at the time.

Chantel was a natural beauty. She stood about five foot five and wore her hair to the back in a neat ponytail that complimented her almond-shaped, hazel eyes. Her measurements were 36-24-37. Her high maintenance décor set her apart from the rest of the females in the club, and that by itself made Speedy want her even more.

"Can I have my hand back, please?" Chantel asked as she slid her hand from his and put it by her side.

Speedy smiled at her conceit just as the bartender returned with the bottles. Speedy figured she was going to play hard to get. He had seen her type around before so he played it cool. He was determined to reel her in one way or the other; he just had to play his hand right. It was the chase that made her interesting to him in the first place.

"Ha, ha, ha!" he laughed as he let her hand go, pulled out a $100 bill, and handed the bartender his tip.

The bartender nodded his head up and down as he cuffed the bill and quickly hid it away before anyone had the chance to see it. He then made his way to the awaiting patrons down the bar.

"Y'all lovely ladies chillin' with us tonight?"

Menace asked as he pointed to the VIP section on the other side of the club.

Red locked eyes with Chantel to let her know she wanted to hang with the two ballers for the night. Speedy noticed the look on Chantel's face and decided to speak up.

"We ain't gonna bite, sexy!" Speedy assured her before he walked off toward the VIP section without waiting for her to respond, even though he was sure she would come.

Chantel's forehead creased with wrinkles, not believing how confident he actually was of himself. She wanted to put him in his place so bad, but truth be told, she was kind of turned on by his arrogance.

"We'll be over in VIP if y'all decide to join us," Menace smiled to Red as he noticed Chantel rolling her eyes at his partner's departing back.

He then walked away, leaving the two women to figure out what they were going to do. Once he was out of earshot, Red began to plead her case.

"So, are we going to chill with them or what?"

She secretly had her fingers crossed behind her

back, hoping Chantel would say yes. Red followed Chantel's eyes and noticed Speedy and Menace with their bottles held high in the air signaling for them to come over to join them in a toast. That only got Red more hyped than she already was.

"Do it for me, Fuzzy," she begged.

Chantel looked over at her friend as she poked out her bottom lip and began to pout. Chantel was never able to tell Red no and really stand by it since they were coming up. After a few blinks of her eyes, Red had Chantel eating out of the palms of her hands.

"Come on, girl!" Chantel gave in, and then let out a long sigh. "You better be glad I love your stinking behind."

Red smiled as she clapped her hands together like a little kid. "I love you too," Red said honestly as she grabbed Chantel by her hand and pulled her toward the VIP section.

She yanked so hard Chantel felt like she caught a slight case of whiplash. Once they reached the red rope that surrounded the VIP section and informed the bouncer who they were with, he led them to Speedy and Menace's booth.

"I see you ladies decided to join the fun." Speedy smiled and stood to his feet as they approach the table.

"Don't flatter yourself!" Chantel shot back as she slid into the booth beside Speedy.

Menace stayed seated, and Red sat beside him with a wide smile on her face. Speedy and Chantel sat quietly while sipping on their drinks and taking in the crowd around them. On the other hand, Menace and Red were deep in conversation while enjoying each other's company. It wasn't until the DJ put on 50 Cent's "In the Club" that Red grabbed Menace by the hand and pulled him out of his seat.

"Come on, cutie, that's my jam!" she shouted over the booming sound system.

She tugged and pulled him all the way to the dance floor until they were in the middle of all the partygoers. Speedy watched as they did their thing. He had to admit that his partner was truly handling his business out there, but Red stole the show with all the exotic moves she was putting on him.

It wasn't until three songs later that Red decided to give Menace a break and return to the booth.

"Anybody want another bottle?" Speedy asked as he turned up his bottle of Moët and finished what little bit he had left.

He then stood to his feet as everyone looked from one to the other before they all declined the offer. Speedy gave himself a once over, making sure everything was still intact before making his way to the VIP exit. Before the bouncer opened the rope to let him out, Speedy turned quickly on heels just in time to catch Chantel eyeing him down. He smiled and winked his eye at her, and then he disappeared into the crowd.

When he finally returned thirty minutes later and a few phone numbers heavier, Chantel was sitting all alone with an annoyed look on her face.

"Damn! She's even sexy when she's mad," he thought to himself as he took his seat.

"Where's Menace and your home girl at?" he questioned, scanning the crowd for the two dancing machines.

"Your friend, whatever his name is, drove Tammie home because she wasn't feeling too good. More than likely, it was all that champagne she had been drinking," Chantel informed him.

"You would have known that if you weren't so busy at the bar chatting with all those little hood rats," she scolded him, shaking her head.

She grabbed her almost empty bottle of Moscato and filled her flute to the rim. Speedy could tell by the slur in her voice that she was feeling the effects from the champagne as well.

"Is that right?" He smiled, noticing the jealous tone of her voice.

He popped the top off of the bottle he held in his hand and then took a sip.

"So how you getting home?" he questioned, once he set the bottle on the table.

Chantel almost spit out the drink she had in her mouth all over the table trying to get the words out.

"I know you are not trying to play me?"

She wiped her mouth, threw the napkin onto the

table, and stood to her feet. Speedy sat back in his seat and threw his hands up in surrender.

"Slow your roll, cowgirl," Speedy laughed as he noticed patrons starting to look over in their direction.

Not realizing she had gotten as loud as she had, Chantel looked around and noticed the same. She slowly began to lower herself back into her seat, feeling a bit embarrassed.

"Not over there! Over here," Speedy demanded as he pointed to the empty seat beside him.

Chantel hesitated before pushing her champagne bottle across the table as she then made her way over beside him. Once she downed the entire glass that was in front of her, she apologized for acting out of character.

"No problem, shorty!" he brushed it off and reached for his bottle to wet his throat.

He slightly brushed her side, and Chantel's body instantly tensed up. Speedy smiled when she closed her eyes and took a deep breath, because he knew that look all too well.

"You ready to bounce?"

Without responding, Chantel finished off her bottle, bobbed her head up and down in agreement, and then grabbed her handbag.

When they got into Speedy's car, Chantel quickly pulled off her heels.

"Ahhh, I can't wait to get in my bed," she whined as she massaged the bottom of her feet.

When she was done, she reclined her seat all the way back and closed her eyes. Speedy glanced down between her legs and wondered what it would feel like to be between them that night.

"Where do you stay?" he asked once they pulled out of the parking lot.

After giving him the directions to her condo, Speedy became even more impressed. About fifteen minutes later he pulled up in front of the upscale complex's parking lot.

"We're here, sleepy head."

Chantel opened her eyes slowly. She couldn't believe she had fallen asleep so quickly. Speedy exited the car and walked over to the passenger side to assist her. She laughed out loud as she stumbled into Speedy's awaiting arms.

"I'm sorry about how I treated you earlier," she apologized as he carried her to the front door.

She fumbled through her handbag for what seemed like an eternity before she found the door key. After she attempted several times to get the door open, Speedy took the key from her, bent down with Chantel still in his arms, and then inserted the key into the hole. He carried her through the threshold of the condo and up a flight of stairs. He figured her bedroom had to be the second one on the right since the first one had slow music playing behind it—not to mention soft moans.

"Ohhhh, Menace!" Speedy heard as he walked by the first door, confirming his suspicions.

Once he entered Chantel's bedroom, Speedy gently laid her down on her king-sized bed and unbuttoned her blouse.

"What are you doing?" she asked as she tried to force her eyes open.

Her heart dropped to the pit of her stomach

when she realized she was too drunk to fight him off if he decided to try to take advantage of her.

"Just relax," Speedy whispered as he slid his hands down to her belt buckle and unloosened her pants.

For some strange reason, she did exactly as she was told. She closed her eyes and raised her backside from off of the bed and let him slide off her pants.

"Speedy," Chantel called out, followed by heavy breathing.

The sight of Chantel in just her bra and thong instantly aroused Speedy. As bad as he wanted her, he couldn't. He liked her too much to take advantage of her in her condition. Chantel became so wet that you could see the moistness seeping through her thong.

"What are you doing?" she asked once Speedy placed her Gucci comforter over her body.

"Not like this," he replied as he leaned down toward her and planted a soft kiss in the middle of her forehead.

Chantel didn't know what to say as she looked up into his eyes. In a way she was disappointed, but on the other hand that moment made her look at Speedy in a different light. She hated that she had judged him earlier without really getting a chance to get to know him ear. *Maybe he is different.*

She sat up in her bed with the covers over the top half of her body as the thought of having sex with someone she only knew for a few hours crossed her mind.

"Don't worry. This is between us." He went into his pocket and pulled out a card with his number on it, and set it on the nightstand beside her bed. "I don't look at you any different," Speedy assured her before he turned his back and walked toward the bedroom door.

Chantel wanted to say something, but she just sat there frozen with tears forming in her eyes.

As soon as Speedy closed the door and turned around to head downstairs, Menace bumped into him as he was coming out of Red's bedroom.

"I was just about to call you to come get me, my

nigga," Menace told him. Once he noticed the glow on Speedy's face, he began with the twenty-one questions. "So, how was it?"

Speedy smiled, shook his head, and then ascended the stairs to the front door.

Menace stayed on his heels the entire way to the car. "It was like dat?" he asked once Speedy never responded.

Speedy opened the car door and stuck his key into the ignition.

"Menace, to tell you the truth, I don't know how it was," Speedy answered honestly, once he started up the car and put it in drive.

Menace looked at his partner in disbelief. As long as he had known him, Speedy never took a female home without beating her back out or getting some head, so Menace knew Speedy was full of shit. Menace let it go, at least for the time being as Speedy hopped back on Highway 301 and headed to Menace's place.

4

It had been two weeks since Chantel let her best friend, Tammie, talk her into going out with her to The Twilight Zone. It if wasn't for the fact that it was Red's twenty-fifth birthday, Chantel would have never in a million years even entertained the thought of going to such a hole-in-the-wall type of club. But she had promised Red she would treat her to any place of her choice, so she felt she was obligated to do so.

It wasn't as bad as she thought it would be though. Truth be told, Chantel was kind of glad she did go. She hadn't been able to stop thinking about Speedy nor his confident swagger, even when she tried to brush him off. She usually had to fight guys off of her, but Speedy proved himself to be much different. There was just something about him that made her want to know more about him. She had even tried to mask her attraction to him by sometimes taking a cold shower to calm her sexual appetite.

"You still ain't gonna tell me what happened between you and ol' boy after the club?" Red interrupted Chantel's thoughts as she drove them to work.

Chantel quickly replied, "His name is Speedy, and like I told you for the thousandth time, nothing ever happened, Red! Why is that so hard for you to believe?" she asked, clearly irritated by her friend's constant questioning.

Red sucked her teeth and then held her mouth sideways. Chantel ignored the gesture and went into her handbag to find her MAC lip gloss. After retrieving it, she pulled down the sun visor, applied the lip gloss, and then rubbed her lips together.

"So, you're gonna stick to that story, huh?"

Even after Red broke down her night of lustful sex with Menace, Chantel still failed to reveal the truth to her friend.

"Tammie! Have I ever lied to you about anything?" Chantel questioned her best friend. "The guy's not even my type."

As long as Red had known Chantel, she was never known to date a guy from the streets other than her high school sweetheart/ex-husband, which ended a few years back, right before Chantel's senior year in college.

"Oh really?" Red asked as she took her eyes off the road to cut them in her friend's direction. "Are we forgetting about Mr. Donte?"

Red focused her eyes back on the road when Chantel didn't respond. She knew the topic of Donte was supposed to be off limits, but she felt Chantel needed to be reminded of where she actually came from.

"That was the old Chantel!" she shot back with an attitude.

Red instantly regretted bringing up the subject, because they had made a vow to never talk about him again as long as they lived. Red planned on making it up to Chantel before the day was over, but for now, they rode the rest of the way to work in complete silence. From the moment Chantel sat down at her desk up until the time she walked into the break room, all she could think about was

Speedy.

"You still mad at me, Fuzzy?" Red asked in a low tone from behind her as Chantel stood at the cappuccino machine fixing herself a cup of coffee.

A smile crept on Chantel's face after hearing her friend's voice. She was feeling kind of bad for the way she flipped on Red, and she couldn't wait for her to come into the break room so she could make up with her best friend.

"Of course not," Chantel answered while turning around with an extra cup of coffee in her hand.

She handed one to Red and proceeded to the table in the back corner that they sat at every day. Red was relieved to hear her friend say those words, and followed behind her to their table. She was also thankful for the coffee; she had already dozed off twice at her desk and couldn't afford another write-up. As soon as Red took the first sip, she immediately spat it back into the cup. Chantel turned around with a victorious grin on her face.

"Now we're even!" Chantel burst into laughter as she looked at the bitter look on Red's face.

"I guess I deserved that!" Red admitted after wiping her mouth with the back of her hand and then joining in on the joke.

She picked up a few packs of sweetener and creamer from the table beside theirs and then added them to her cup. Once they were seated, Chantel ran down what happened between her and Speedy, from the time he returned from the bar, to him taking her home, down to him undressing her and putting her in bed without even trying to have sex with her. Red sat there wide-eyed and speechless as she observed every word and detail. She couldn't believe what a gentleman Speedy had turned out to be.

"He must really like you, Fuzzy," Red assured her with dreamy eyes.

She sat with her elbows propped on the table with her face resting in the palms of her hands. That thought had crossed Chantel's mind several times before, but her past relationship wouldn't allow her to call him. Red could see the expression on Chantel's face change, and she felt that she needed to speak up.

"Look, Fuzzy! You can't go on comparing your

failed relationship with Donte with every man you meet. Whether you want to believe it or not, there are some good men still out there."

Chantel looked into Red's eyes but didn't respond. She knew Red was telling the truth.

"Don't let that fine-ass nigga slip away from you." Red smiled as she put her hand on top of Chantel's.

"You know what, girl? You're right! I'm going to step out of the box and give him a call when we get off of work," Chantel assured her friend.

Their girl talk was interrupted by their supervisor announcing over the loud speaker that it was time to get back to work.

As Red drove home, Chantel sat on the passenger side fumbling with the card that Speedy left on her nightstand.

"Call him," Red demanded.

Red was more excited for Chantel than she was. Chantel took out her cell phone and dialed his number. After Speedy agreed to meet her at Big Mama's Kitchen, Chantel hung up and told Red the good news. As soon as Red pulled up into their apartment complex parking lot, Chantel darted toward her car.

"Good luck!" Red called out to her friend as she entered her car.

Chantel waved her hand in the air with a big smile on her face as she pulled out of the parking lot and headed to meet her knight in shining armor.

* * *

"Yo, why in the hell you standing there with a big-ass Kool-Aid smile on your face?" Menace asked as he stared at his friend.

Speedy stood in the middle of the living room floor staring at the phone in his hand. He had been waiting on a call from Chantel for two weeks now, and it finally came.

"That was shorty from the club the other week," Speedy replied as he looked at his watch to check the time.

He had fifteen minutes to make it to Big Mama's Kitchen if he didn't want to be late.

"Word?" Menace asked surprised. "So what's the deal?"

Menace took a seat on the loveseat in front of

the television and began to channel surf. After landing on BET, Menace pulled out a blunt he had been smoking on earlier and re-lit it.

"She asked me if I wanted to join her for dinner at Big Mama's Kitchen," Speedy informed his partner.

"So, whatcha gonna do?" Menace inhaled, let out a huge cloud of smoke, and then handed it to Speedy.

"I'm good," Speedy declined as he put on his jacket. "I got a hot date to attend."

He popped his collar, pulled out his car keys, and then headed toward the door.

"Pussy whipped muthafucka!" Menace mumbled as Speedy reached for the door.

"I heard that, nigga," Speedy shot back as he opened the front door. Right before he closed it behind him, he said, "Told you I didn't hit it." He then slammed the door shut.

"Well, you should have," Menace yelled through the closed door loud enough for Speedy to hear him.

Speedy was at his car when the same ol' white

crackhead from a few weeks ago pulled up to the curb in front of the spot.

"You got a fifty?" he asked as Speedy opened the door to his car.

"Nah! Go knock on the door. The guy inside will take care of you," he instructed him before hopping in his car.

"My man," the crackhead declared as he turned on his heels and rushed up to the front door of the spot to get his afternoon fix.

Speedy shook his head as he watched the crackhead almost fall at least twice before reaching his destination.

"Crack is a muthafucka," Speedy laughed before he put his Lex coupe in drive and peeled out.

* * *

Speedy pulled up to Big Mama's Kitchen ten minutes later. He spotted Chantel as soon as he walked into the place. She stood to her feet when she saw him, and she began to wave him over to her table. On his way over to the table, he noticed how pretty she was even without makeup.

"I see you found the place," Chantel said as she

56

gave him a warming hug.

"Wowwww! Is this the same woman from the other night?" Speedy joked as he stepped back and looked her up and down.

He was really surprised at how she was acting.

"Yes, it is." She smiled. "Stop making me feel bad." She poked out her lip. "I just thought you were one of those guys."

Speedy stopped her before she could finish her sentence, by putting his pointer finger to her lips. "Never judge a book by its cover. No apologies needed, beautiful," he stated as he removed his finger. "I'm willing to start over if you are."

"I would like that," Chantel admitted while looking into his eyes.

"Hi, my name is Speedy." He extended his hand to her.

"Hi, I'm Chan," she began, before catching herself and starting over. "I mean, hi, my name is Fuzzy. Nice to meet you."

Speedy smiled and then took her hand in his. Chantel wanted to continue fighting her feelings toward Speedy, but she couldn't deny her attraction to him anymore. Just as she was about to speak, the waiter came to take their order.

"I'll give you two another moment," the waiter announced as he saw the sparks flying between them.

Once he was gone, Speedy spoke up.

"So now I get the privilege of calling you Fuzzy, huh?" he asked as he picked up the menu and began looking through it.

"You have a problem with that?" she questioned as she picked up a menu and did the same.

"Not at all." Speedy smiled.

After finding what he wanted to order, he then shook his head from side to side.

"Stop it, will you? I know I wasn't that bad the other night," Fuzzy said.

Speedy raised his eyebrow and wrinkled his forehead.

"You're making me feel bad."

They both burst into laughter just as the waiter came back to take their orders.

After they ate and got to know each other a little better, they felt like they had known each other a lifetime. To Speedy's surprise, when the waiter returned with the bill, Chantel informed Speedy she was going to pay for the meal. Speedy tried to protest, but Chantel wasn't having it: "You can pay for the next one."

He smiled thinking there was going to be a next date after all.

"Thank you very much," the waiter smiled and then took Chantel's black card to ring up their meal.

When he returned, Speedy and Chantel made their way to the parking lot. They stood at Chantel's car and stared at each other for a second. The moment was awkward.

"No it don't," Speedy said, breaking the silence.

"Excuse me?"

"You were wondering if our time together has to end right now, so I answered the question you wanted to ask."

Chantel looked at Speedy in disbelief because that's exactly what she was thinking. "Well, since you're a mind reader, what am I thinking right now?"

Speedy smiled, leaned in closer, and then placed

his lips on hers.

Fuzzy closed her eyes, wrapped her arms around Speedy's neck, and put her tongue down his throat.

"Whew!" she said out loud as she fanned her face to cool herself off.

"Was I correct?" Speedy asked with confidence.

"No! I was actually thinking about going to Toisnot Park and taking a walk, but believe me when I tell you, I really enjoyed the kiss."

They both started laughing and decided to take their date to her place to watch a movie and relax instead.

* * *

Halfway through the second movie, Speedy received a phone call.

"Yo!" he answered, half asleep.

"You have a collect call from Menace. To accept, please press 5. To decline, please press—"

Speedy immediately pressed 5 before the recording even finished.

"Yo, what the fuck you doing in jail?" Speedy asked as he sat up on the couch, awaking Fuzzy from her resting spot on his chest.

"I can't talk right now, but I need for you to come and bail me out before I bust a nigga's head in dis bitch," Menace threatened.

Inmates heard him loud and clear but dared not to say anything for fear of their well-being.

"I'll get dat change right back to you when I touch down," Speedy dismissed what Menace just said and spoke up quickly. "No need for all dat, brute. I got you. I'll be there ASAP."

Speedy ended their call as Fuzzy looked on.

"What's wrong, Speedy?" she asked.

Without breaking his pace, Speedy replied, "Pass me the phonebook. I need to get in touch with a bondsman so I can bail Menace out of jail," he answered as he scrambled to put his shirt on.

"I'm coming." Fuzzy jumped up and grabbed a pair of sweats and slid them on over her boy shorts as Speedy slid on his Timbs. She made her way to the bathroom to brush her teeth.

"Yo, where's your phonebook?" Speedy asked for the second time, becoming impatient of Fuzzy's slow movement.

"I got you, bae," she called out from the

bathroom with a mouth full of toothpaste.

When she finished, she came out and put on a pair of shoes, ready to go handle the task at hand.

"Your car or mine?" Fuzzy wanted to know as they headed toward the front door.

"I guess I can drive while you look up a bondsman," he informed while leading the way out the door.

Fuzzy had a confused look on her face once they reached his car. "Speedy."

He paused before opening his door.

"I told you that I got you, didn't I?"

"I heard you, Fuzzy," he replied as he opened up the car door and got in.

Fuzzy shook her head, got in the car, and then put on her seatbelt. When Speedy pulled out of the parking lot, he noticed that Fuzzy didn't have the phonebook in her hand.

"Where's the phonebook? I told you I needed you to look up a bondsman for Menace."

Speedy was clearly irritated at that point.

"Speedy. That's what I've been trying to tell you for the longest time. I'm a bondsman."

Speedy looked at Fuzzy in disbelief.

"It's a long story, but I promise I'll tell you everything when we get back home."

Speedy focused his attention back on the road. Within twenty minutes they were pulling up at the police station. Speedy stayed outside in the car while Fuzzy went in to handle all of the paper work to get Menace released.

Once Menace was released, Speedy and Fuzzy dropped him off at The spot to get his car. Before Speedy and Menace parted ways, they promised to get up first thing in the morning, because they didn't want to talk about their business in the presence of a stranger.

When Speedy and Fuzzy made it back to her place, she told him everything about herself— from how she met her ex-husband, Donte, in high school, to him putting her through college, down to him convincing her to become a bondsman. Through their long conversation that night, Speedy learned that she had been constantly cheated on by Donte, which eventually led to their divorce. They talked until the wee hours of the morning, and Speedy held her tight as she emptied her deepest secrets on him. He listened to every word. He had no idea she had been through so much in her young life, and he made a vow to himself that he would never do anything to hurt her nor allow anyone to violate her ever again. Before they knew it, they had fallen asleep in each other's arms.

* * *

"Time to get up, babe," Fuzzy called out in a cheerful tone as she stood over Speedy with a breakfast tray in her hand.

Speedy opened his eyes and looked around trying to focus his sight on his surroundings.

"Damn," he silently cursed himself when it dawned on him that he had stayed the night over at Fuzzy's house.

"What time is it?" he asked once he remembered that he took off his watch before he lay down.

"It's almost noon," Fuzzy answered.

Speedy sat up and wiped the crust from his eyes. She sat the tray of food onto his lap and then took a seat beside him.

"I didn't know if you ate pork or not, so I cooked

you some turkey bacon instead of pork."

Speedy glanced at the cheese eggs and grits, and couldn't wait to tear into them. Just as he was about to pick up the fork and dig in, Fuzzy grabbed it and began feeding him.

"There's a bath rag, toothbrush, and a towel waiting for you on the bathroom sink," she instructed while filling his mouth with grits.

After she finished feeding him, she took the tray into the kitchen while Speedy went into the bathroom to straighten himself up. The entire time he was taking a shower, Speedy was thinking of a lie to tell Tawana for staying out all night without even calling her. He knew he was in for a cursing out, when he noticed that his battery had died on his cell when he looked at the display screen. He could only imagine how many times Tawana had called him throughout the night. He was too afraid to check his voicemail. Only God knew the crazy messages she had surely left on it.

After Speedy got dressed and entered the living room, Fuzzy, Red, and Menace were all waiting for him.

"What's up, Sleeping Beauty?" Menace joked as he stood up from the couch that he was sitting on to show his partner some love.

"I thought Chantel was holding you hostage, so I had to come by and see if you needed any help getting out of her grasp," Menace teased as he looked over at Chantel, who stood there with her arms crossed over her chest with a big smile on her face.

"Nah, it ain't even like dat. My battery died on my cell last night," Speedy informed his partner. "I was just about to go by the spot to check on you," he assured Menace. "I'm about to bounce and check up on a few things. I'll call you once I charge my phone up to check on you," he addressed Fuzzy before giving her a hug.

"Okay," she replied, and then went in for a kiss. "Don't have me waiting on your call all day neither." Fuzzy blushed as she balled her fist and raised it in the air at him.

Red and Menace stared at the both of them, not believing their eyes.

"What?" Fuzzy asked as she looked at the two,

before she grabbed Speedy by his hand and walked him to the front door.

"Awe," Red and Menace said in unison as they followed behind the couple.

"Haters," Fuzzy whispered to Speedy once she let his hand go to open the door.

"Thanks for making my bail last night, Chantel," Menace said with appreciation.

He was truly thankful, because he knew if he would have had to stay overnight, somebody would've felt his wrath.

"No problem," she assured him as Speedy and Menace made their way to their cars. "Just know you owe me one!" She winked her eye as she cleared her throat.

"No doubt. I got you."

"Oh yeah," Speedy interrupted. "I guess that gives you the right to call her Fuzzy now," he joked as he looked over the roof of his car at his partner.

"I'm glad you gave him permission to call you Fuzzy," Menace told Chantel as he looked from his partner to her.

Fuzzy stood paralyzed and wide-eyed while she

tried to think of a response.

"My bad!" Menace told her after realizing he had stuck his foot in his mouth.

Speedy looked at Fuzzy, who shrugged hers shoulders and gave him her innocent girl look in return.

"Man, I was getting tired of trying to remember to call you Chantel when I was around him," Menace admitted.

"Y'all got that one!" Speedy told them as he got into his car and pulled off while smiling.

5

When Speedy walked into his house, he could hear Tawana in the bedroom laughing. Since she was in such a good mood, he hoped that would take some of the sting off of the tongue-lashing he was sure he was about to receive once she found out he was home.

The closer he got to the room door, the louder her laughter became. The door was slightly ajar, so he slowly stuck his head inside.

"Let me hit you back later," she told the caller on the other end when she saw Speedy's face. But her smile faded once she placed her phone on the bed, and she jumped straight into bitch mode. "Where the fuck you been all night?" she screamed as she stood up from the bed and walked up in his face.

"I had some business that needed to be attended to," he quickly replied as he walked past her and made his way into the closet to find an outfit to put on.

Tawana marched into the closet after him.

"All night long, Marcus?" she shouted as she stood behind him with her arms folded across her chest. "It must look like I got the word stupid written all across my forehead or something," she continued, breathing heavily. "You at least could have had the respect to call me to tell me something." Tawana was just about in tears. "You can't even say nothing, huh? Oh, let me guess. Your phone died?"

"Huh, you're right for once. As a matter of fact, my phone did die, see."

Speedy placed his cell in her face showing her that his phone was actually dead, but she wasn't buying it. Tawana instantly slapped his phone and hand out of her face, almost making him drop it on the floor.

"Marcus, don't try to play me. I'm not one of those little hood-rat bitches in the streets that you're used to dealing with. You gonna fuck around and lose the best thing you ever had," she threatened, before she turned around and stormed out of the closet.

She didn't stop until she made it out the door and to her car. Speedy didn't even bother to go after her. He knew exactly where she was going, because every time she got mad at him, she would storm off to her sister's house to vent their problems to her. When Speedy walked out of the closet, the first thing he noticed was that Tawana had left her cell phone on the bed. He knew she would be back to get her lifeline as soon as she noticed she didn't have it, so he intended on being gone before she returned to duck part two of his tongue-lashing that he knew would come.

Just as he was about to walk out of the room, Tawana's Blackberry began to ring. He figured it was Tawana calling him to tell him to bring her cellular over to Crystal's house whenever he came out, so he didn't even bother to check the caller ID before he answered.

"What?" he asked in an annoyed tone.

He looked at the display screen when he got no response.

He noticed that the caller was still on the phone, so he put his ear back to it.

"Hello," he asked again, before the line finally went dead.

He locked the number in his mental Rolodex, and then scrolled through the list of people she had recently called, to check the last number she had dialed. Speedy grew angry thinking it had to be a guy calling, since the caller hung up when he answered her phone. He tried calling back the number several times but got no answer. Even after he blocked the number, no one still answered the phone.

Speedy threw Tawana's cell back on the bed, took his battery off the charger, and then hooked it up to the back of his phone. He was about to go over to Tawana's sister's house to question her about the strange number, when he heard her entering the house. She had a look of concern on her face when they locked eyes.

"What? Did you forget something?" he asked as she walked passed him.

Tawana breathed a sigh of relief when she noticed her cell phone in the exact spot she had left it. She walked over, retrieved it from the bed, and placed it in her handbag. When she turned around, she saw the strange expression Speedy had on his face, and she felt a chill run up and down her spine.

"What?" she asked when he stopped her from getting by him.

"What, my ass!" he shouted. "Who in the fuck were you on the phone with when I came in earlier?"

He could tell she was trying to think of a lie to tell him when she started to look in every other direction besides his face.

"When?" she stuttered, trying to buy herself some more time.

Little did she know that was the worst thing she could do. Out of nowhere, Speedy backhanded her and sent her flying across the bed and onto the floor. She picked herself up, holding her swollen bottom lip as blood trickled from it.

"What is wrong with you, Marcus?" Tawana asked as tears trailed her cheeks.

Out of all the years she and Speedy had been together, not once had he ever raised a hand to strike her, until now.

"I'm only gonna ask you one more time who you were on the phone with when I came home, Tawana!" Speedy warned as he stood over her with his fist balled up.

She could tell by the fire that burned within his eyes that he meant what he said. She realized that whether she decided to tell the truth or a lie to save her ass, the outcome would not be pretty.

"I'm sorry, Marcus," she began, deciding to come clean with the truth. "It was nothing," Tawana promised as she began crying hysterically.

Speedy could feel his heart breaking into a thousand pieces as he anticipated the worst. He knew whatever came out of her mouth next would change their lives forever.

"It only happened once."

A single tear fell from his eye as she confirmed

his thoughts. All he could do was look on in disbelief and shake his head from side to side, not wanting to believe what he had just heard.

"Please don't," she begged as Speedy backpedaled through their room door and into the hallway. "Wait," she called out as she picked herself up off the floor.

"I'll be back to get all of my shit later," Speedy shouted before exiting the house.

Tawana broke down in tears when she heard the front door slam shut behind him. She had a bad feeling that he was gone out of her life when she heard the loud screeching of his tires as he drove out of the parking lot. She just hoped he wasn't gone out of her life for good.

6

Speedy rode around in his car for hours as rain drops tap-danced on his windshield. He wound up outside of Fuzzy's apartment complex, until he built up enough courage to go and knock on her door.

"Who is it?" Fuzzy yelled as she slid on a nightgown and ascended the stairs.

She looked out the peep hole and saw Speedy standing there with tears in his eyes. She snatched the door open, jumped in his arms, and began kissing him passionately, trying to take some of his pain away. When he put her back down, she led the way to her bedroom. No words were exchanged as she stood in front of him, took off his coat, and unbuttoned his shirt. She ran her fingers up and down his bare chest, and then stopped them on his stomach. Fuzzy unhooked his belt buckle and watched as his pants fell to the floor. Once he stepped out of them, Fuzzy backed up and slid off her nightgown. Speedy tried to speak, but Fuzzy prevented him by putting her tongue back down his throat. She didn't want anything to be said that might spoil their moment. She pushed him backward onto her bed and made her way on top of him. She bit down on her bottom lip as Speedy made his way inside her love nest. He had never experienced a place as warm and wet as he was at the time. They made intense love all through the night until the early morning sunrise, relieving themselves of the pent-up emotions they had held deep inside. They both cried for different reasons, but the most important thing was that they were there for each other when they needed each other the most.

* * *

"Wake up, Fuzzy!" Speedy shook her until she was half awake.

"What's wrong?" she asked as she focused her sight on the fully dressed Speedy. "What time is it?"

She stretched and yawned as she tried to gather her strength. She smiled at the slight tingling sensation between her legs.

"Nothing's wrong. It's nine o'clock and I got something to show you," he replied, waiting for her to make an attempt to get out of bed. "Get dressed. I'll be downstairs waiting for you," Speedy informed her as he exited the bedroom.

So much for a morning quickie, Fuzzy thought to herself before she rolled out of bed and made her way to the bathroom.

Speedy was watching CNN when Fuzzy emerged from her bedroom and into the living room.

"So, where we going?" she asked cheerfully.

She loved surprises, and she was sure that whatever Speedy had in store for her that day, she was going to enjoy every minute of it.

"Don't ask no questions. Just come with me," he demanded as he held out his hand for Fuzzy to join him.

He led the way out of the apartment and to his car.

After about fifteen minutes of riding in silence,

Fuzzy's curiosity began to get the best of her. "Okay, Speedy. You know this is killing me, don't you?" she asked while looking over at him.

He didn't say a word.

"You can at least give me a clue," Fuzzy insisted.

"You'll see in a few minutes. We're almost there."

Speedy turned the radio up a notch and let the soft voice of Sade permeate the air as he sang along: "This is no ordinary love, no ordinary love."

Fuzzy smiled as she shook her head, reclined her seat, and then slid her Chanel frames over her eyes.

It took another twenty minutes before they were finally pulling up to their destination.

"Wake up. We're here," Speedy announced as he turned the engine off and looked over at Fuzzy.

She removed her shades from her eyes and began to look around.

"This is nice," she exclaimed as Speedy made his way around the car to the passenger's door to help her out.

Once he shut the door behind her, they made their way up the semicircular driveway to the huge colonial-style home.

"Whose house is this?" she asked once they reached the front door.

"It's mine," Speedy replied as he pulled out another set of keys and stuck one in the door to unlock it.

The door swung open and Speedy invited her in. "Are you coming or not?"

Fuzzy slowly entered behind him and was at a loss for words at what she saw. It was like she was watching *Lifestyles of the Rich and Famous* as her eyes scanned the spacious entrance.

"Let me show you around," he offered as they walked down the long hallway.

Halfway down, Fuzzy stopped in her tracks and stared at the exotic fish swimming in the aquarium that was built into the wall of the hallway.

"You ain't seen nothing yet," Speedy boasted as he led the way to the living room.

"I've always wanted one of these," Fuzzy

claimed as she walked over to the bricked-in fireplace on the far side of the room.

Speedy stood at the door while Fuzzy went over to the grand piano and played a few notes.

"I didn't know you knew how to play the piano!"

Speedy was truly amazed at her talent.

"Yeah. My father made me take lessons when I was a little girl."

He noticed how her once happy features quickly saddened when she talked about her father. She stood up and walked over to the all-white Italian sectional and ran her fingers across the expensive piece. For the first time, Fuzzy took a look around and noticed everything in the entire room was white.

She glanced up at Speedy, and it was at that very moment that she knew there was something special about him, and she was going to do everything in her power to bring it out of him.

"This is so beautiful," Fuzzy admitted as she walked up to him and placed her lips on his.

"Thanks! But the next time I need you to do me

one favor," he told her as they headed down the hallway to finish off the rest of the tour.

"And what's that?"

"The next time you enter the white room, I'ma need you to take off your shoes," he laughed.

Feeling totally embarrassed, Fuzzy put both hands over her mouth and then mumbled, "Why didn't you tell me?"

Speedy just smiled and led the way up the stairwell to the second floor.

"This is where the king sleeps," Speedy joked before opening the door to the master bedroom.

Fuzzy couldn't believe what she was seeing. Everything in the room was black and trimmed in gold, even the two ceiling fans. The thing that intrigued her the most was the huge circular king-sized bed that sat in the center of the room. She ran straight to it, turned around, and then flopped onto it backward into the dozens of pillows that sat on top of it. Speedy just laughed and then grabbed the remote off of one of the nearby nightstands and pressed a few buttons. Immediately, the bed began to turn in a slow merry-go-round motion. Fuzzy felt like a kid at the playground as she watched herself spin around and around in the mirrors on the ceiling above.

"I've died and gone to heaven," she whispered before she closed her eyes and enjoyed the feeling.

Speedy hit another button on the remote and the bed came to a stop. "You are too much."

Fuzzy stood to her feet and made her way to the mahogany doors that led to the balcony. When she stepped out onto it, she inhaled a deep breath of fresh air and took in the forest's natural beauty that surrounded the residence. She looked down, and a smile came to her face as she pictured herself swimming in the Olympic-sized pool below.

"I love this place, Speedy," Fuzzy admitted as she held her arms up high and backed into the room toward him.

"Is that right?" he asked as she turned around to face him.

"Yep!" she answered as she planted a kiss on his lips.

"That's good to know."

Once she faced him, she noticed he was holding an extra set of keys in his hand. Her eyes grew wide and her hands quickly shot to her mouth while she was trying to hold in her screams.

"Don't play with me, Speedy," Fuzzy warned as she looked into his eyes to see if he was playing some type of joke on her.

"Well, if you don't want them."

He attempted to put them back in his pocket, but she snatched them from him so fast that he almost lost a finger. She ran down the stairs to the front door to see if they actually fit the lock. After unlocking and locking the door several times, she was convinced. When she turned around, Speedy was standing right behind her. Fuzzy jumped into his arms with tears in her eyes.

"You're too good to be true," she told him in between kisses.

When he finally put her back down, he let her know the one main rule if she wanted to stay. "Never tell anyone where this house is. I mean anyone, Fuzzy," Speedy warned as he looked her deep in her eyes.

After agreeing to his term, Fuzzy and Speedy made love throughout the house, including outside in the pool area. After taking a shower, Fuzzy lay in the bed with Speedy with her back to him.

"Who are these people?" she asked as she picked up the framed picture of a man and woman from the nightstand. "They look so happy."

It was a picture of his mother and father at what seemed like a party of some type. Speedy knew what picture she was referring to, but he looked over her shoulder anyway to get a glimpse of it.

"That's my mother and father the night they got killed by a drunk driver after their fifteen-year anniversary," he answered.

"I'm so sorry," she replied in a surprised manner while putting it back in its rightful place.

She turned around to face him and wiped away the tears from his eyes, wishing she could take the pain from them. When he got himself together, Speedy broke down his entire family history. Fuzzy could relate because her father was also at a high level of the drug trade and had been taken away from her. Once she told him how close she was with her father, he understood why her expression changed when she was playing the piano.

They talked about everything into the wee hours of the night until they fell asleep in each other's arms. Once they woke up in the morning, they made love again.

7

After Speedy and Menace hooked up the cameras at the spot, they began to bag up the work.

"So what's the lawyer talking about?" Speedy asked as he glanced over at his partner.

Ever since Menace caught his sell charge, they hadn't talked much about the time he was facing, so Speedy decided now was as good a time as any to catch up on the subject. Menace stopped bagging up and then let out a long and dreadful sigh before responding. "Man, that cracker's talking about twenty-four to thirty months because of a nigga's priors," Menace said as he reached into his pocket and retrieved a ziplock back full of dro.

Speedy just shook his head.

"Damn, dawg! What if we throw his ass an extra G or two?" Speedy offered, not wanting to accept what he had just heard.

"Psssss! You know I already tried that, my

nigga! He's talkin' about that punk-ass officer who's got it in for me for some reason or another, so the DA wasn't budging on my plea agreement. The only other option is to roll over on a muthafucka, and you know that ain't in my blood."

Speedy agreed with his partner as he patted his pockets for the blunts.

"Come on, nigga! Don't tell me you forgot the blunts?" Menace asked as he threw the ziplock bag onto the coffee table in front of him.

Speedy reached in his pocket and pulled out a penny.

"Heads or tails?" Speedy asked as he tossed the coin up in the air.

"Tails," Menace chose.

Speedy caught the penny in his hand and slammed it on the backside of this other hand. Speedy then lifted his hand and cursed when he saw it was tails. He put the coin back in his pocket and then headed toward the door.

As soon as he walked out, he inhaled the stale air and looked around. Then he made his way across the front yard and opened the fence. Two teenagers walked by when he closed it behind him.

"Hey, yo!" he called out to the two teens.

They stopped in their tracks and looked at him.

"How would y'all like to make a couple of dollars?"

"What you want for us to do?" the tall slim teen asked.

But before Speedy could reply, the short dark teen interrupted. "Yo! What you need, big homie? I got you. You don't gotta give me shit."

Speedy nodded his head and smiled. He then dug into his pocket to find a $20, but all he had were $50s and $100s.

"Here!" Speedy offered the kid the $100 just to test his loyalty.

He then told him what he wanted from the store. The dark-skinned kid took the bill, and he and his partner headed in the direction of the store down the block. Speedy turned on his heels and headed back to the spot to finish bagging up his work.

"Yo, who is that?" Menace asked, when he heard someone knocking on the door ten minutes later.

Speedy looked at the monitor before he answered.

"Oh, it's the kids I sent to the store for the blunts," Speedy replied. He stood to his feet and made his way over to the door to let them in. "You got that for me, kid?" he asked the dark-skinned teen as he welcomed them into the spot.

"No doubt!" the dark-skinned teen replied as he handed Speedy the box of blunts.

Speedy smiled and then threw the box of blunts to Menace, who quickly caught them and opened them. The dark skin teen offered Speedy the $100 bill that he gave him earlier to pay for the box of blunts.

"Yo, how did you pay for the blunts?" Speedy asked as he shot a glance at Menace and then back at the teens.

He hoped they didn't steal them, because the last thing he wanted was for the police to be coming around for some stolen blunts.

"I bought them," the teen informed them as he pulled out a wad of money and flashed Speedy.

It was no more than $500 crumpled up, but

Speedy was impressed at how the young teen carried himself.

"What's your name, kid?"

"Lil Man!" the kid replied with confidence as he held his head up high.

Lil Man was sixteen years old and stood about five foot six. His skin tone was dark chocolate, and his hair was jet black and wavy. He always kept a serious look on his face that made him look older beyond his young years. The scar that he carried under his left eye told a story of its own.

"And who's your homie?" Menace asked, when he finished rolling the blunt and put it between his lips.

He flicked the lighter twice before Lil Man's friend answered.

"I'm Lucky," the other teen announced, looking over in Menace's direction.

For some strange reason, Menace took a liking to the tall, light-skinned kid.

"You gonna let me hit dat shit or what?" Lucky asked as he made his way over to Menace and stood in front of him.

"I like this kid already," Menace admitted, sliding over so Lucky could take a seat beside him.

Speedy and Menace watched as Lucky removed the small .22 from the small of his back before taking his seat. Menace bobbed his head up and down before taking one last pull off the blunt, and then handed it to him. Lucky took a long and deep pull of the potent weed like a seasoned vet without choking on it even once.

By the end of their smoke session, Speedy and Menace had taken Lil Man and Lucky under their wings and became their suppliers. Lil Man and Lucky's job was to be the lookout for them in the daytime while they sold their work, and whenever they left, Lil Man and Lucky could post up in the spot.

The teens readily agreed because they knew Speedy and Menace had the best work in the hood, because as long as they were around, no one else was able to get off of their packs. That was the opportunity the young teens had been looking for, and they were going to take full advantage of it.

8

Speedy pulled up to the house that he and Tawana once shared, for the first time in months. He hadn't even spoken a word to her since the day he left her crying. She had been constantly calling and texting him, but he never responded back to her. She would leave voice messages on his cell telling him that it was very important that they talked ASAP. It was a Monday afternoon when he finally gave in and decided to return one of her calls, and they agreed to meet at the house.

He let himself in and unwanted memories rushed his brain once the aroma of cucumber melon body spray assaulted his nose.

Damn! I gotta hurry up and get the rest of my shit! Speedy thought to himself as he made his way to his old bedroom.

When he walked into the room, he noticed everything was almost as he had left it, besides the unmade bed. He walked across the room to the bedroom closet to check his shoe boxes. He smiled when he opened each one of them and saw the neatly stacked bills in their proper places. He made his way a little deeper to see if the money in the safe was still intact. His heart raced with anticipation as he put in the last digit and gave the handle a tug.

"It's all there," Tawana promised, leaning against the door jam.

Speedy swiftly turned his head in her direction.

"You're gonna get enough of sneaking up on somebody," Speedy said.

He turned his attention back to his safe and began to pull out stack after stack of $100s, placing them into a Gucci duffel bag that set beside him. Tears began to well up in Tawana's eyes as she firmly gripped her stomach. She fought back tears as she watched Speedy pack up all his belongings. A sense of nausea came over her and her knees began to get weak, so she made her way over to the bed and took a seat on the edge of it.

Once Speedy was finished, he walked out of the

closet and stood in front of her. As much as he hated to admit it, he still truly loved her. If it weren't for her betrayal, he would have quickly forgiven her for her mistake.

"I paid the lease up for the next six months," he informed her as he put his finger under her chin so she could look at his face.

She looked into his eyes and shook her head.

"I want you to come back home," Tawana confessed as she grabbed his hand, kissed the back of it, and laid it against her cheek.

"I hope that ain't what was so important that you kept blowing my phone up," he said, removing his hand from her face.

She couldn't believe he could be so heartless toward her after all they had been through together. He acted as if all the years that they had shared meant absolutely nothing. Tawana looked up at Speedy in disbelief.

"As a matter of fact, no! That's not why I was so-called blowing up your phone, as you call it," she screamed while rolling her eyes at him. "You know what, Marcus? Don't even worry about it because I'm good. I don't need you. Just take your shit and leave."

Tawana got up and ran to the bathroom and slammed the door behind her. No longer able to hold the contents in her stomach, she lifted up the toilet seat, bent her head down, and threw up her lunch.

"You all right?" Speedy asked with concern.

He walked to the bathroom door and listened to her heaving on the other side.

"Just leave!" she yelled as she wiped the corner of her mouth.

"I left a shoe box with money in it. There should be a little over $10,000 in it," Speedy assured her.

"I don't want shit from you, Mar—!" she tried to say, but was cut short by her vomiting.

When Speedy turned to leave, he looked at the shoe box filled with money on the closet floor. He knew she didn't mean what she said about the money, so he walked past it and made his way out of the bedroom. When he got to the front door, he took the house key off of his key ring and set it on the coffee table beside the door. He looked back at the bedroom and wiped the single tear from his eye before he made his exit.

Twenty minutes into the ride back to his house, Speedy received a text from Tawana that read: "I'm pregnant. That's what was so important."

After Speedy read the text, he pulled his car over to the side of the highway to read it again to make sure he read it correctly the first time. He tried calling her, but he only got her voicemail. After the third attempt, Speedy decided to block his number and then call her. As soon as Tawana heard his voice, she immediately hung up.

"Damn!" he cursed himself, before he jumped back onto the highway, made a U-turn, and headed back to her place.

When he pulled back up, he jumped out and raced to the front door. He searched his key ring for the house key before remembering he left it on the coffee table beside the door.

"Open up, Tawana!" he demanded as he pounded on it repeatedly.

"Go away!" she cried, leaning her forehead against the door frame.

"I'm not going anywhere until you let me in so we can talk!"

Tawana lifted her head and stared at the door, dumbfounded. "Oh, now you want to talk, huh, Marcus!" she yelled, before hitting the door as hard as she could. "What about when I wanted to talk for the past couple of weeks, Marcus?"

It was then that Speedy realized what an ass he had been for not even seeing what Tawana had wanted all of those times. Guilt started to sink in when the thought of not being there for her when she really needed him.

"I'm so sorry, Tawana. I can't change what happened in the past, but I'm here now and ready to listen," Speedy promised. "Just open the door so we can talk, please."

Tawana stood on the other side of the door quietly. She wanted so badly for Speedy to hold her and tell her that everything was going to be all right, but she knew it wouldn't be that simple. Tawana let out a deep sigh before responding. "I need for you to promise me that you won't get mad at me, Marcus," she said with a slight shiver in her tone.

The thought of Speedy striking her again completely terrified her.

"Why would I get made at—?" Speedy began before stopping in mid-sentence. He thought about what she was asking of him and tried to keep his cool before speaking again. "Baby, just open the door!"

Tawana wiped her eyes and debated on whether or not to open the door for him.

"Open the fuckin' door!" Speedy demanded, unable to hold in his anger.

He began kicking and punching the door, almost knocking it off its hinges. Tawana let out a loud scream before backing away from it.

"Marcus, I'm calling the police!" she warned, before she pulled out her cell phone and dialed 911.

Her hands shook uncontrollably as she hit the speaker button so Speedy could hear the operator.

"Hello. What's your emergency?" the operator

asked.

Tears trailed down Tawana's cheeks as she answered. "I think someone is trying to get into my home," she responded between sniffs.

"What's your address, ma'am. I'll send a patrol car over as soon as possible."

"It's 1604," was all Speedy needed to hear before he turned around and headed to his car. As soon as he sat down in the driver's seat, it started pouring down raining.

"Fuck!" he cursed as he slammed his fist against the steering wheel several times.

He glanced up at the apartment and wondered where things went so wrong between them, before starting the car.

Tawana stared out her bedroom window as she disconnected the call with the operator. Little did Speedy know, but Tawana wondered the same thing as his taillights disappeared in the distance.

9

Speedy, Menace, Lil Man, and Lucky all sat on the front steps of the spot in what they called a "cipher" as they passed around three blunts at a time. This was something that became a daily routine after they joined forces. Things had been going good the past couple of months for the crew. Money had been flowing hand over fist, and Speedy and Menace owed it all to Lil Man and Lucky. The spot had been popping 24/7 since the youngsters had been pulled into the mix.

"Next Friday's the big day," Menace announced to Speedy as he passed him a blunt.

Time was going by so fast that Speedy didn't realize until just then that Menace's court date was right around the corner.

"Damn! I hate that cracker!" Speedy admitted before he took two tokes of the marijuana smoke and then passed it to Lil Man.

Before Menace got the chance to speak on the subject, an unmarked undercover car pulled up in front of the spot.

"If it ain't my good ol' friend, Menace," Detective Russo stated proudly, with an evil grin on his face.

Joey Russo was a white up-and-coming undercover agent, but after making the arrest of Menace and a few more local hustlers, he became a second-in-command detective. That wasn't hard for him to do since his constant use of cocaine, crack, and heroin gave him the natural look of a true addict.

"Fuck you, pig!" Menace shot back as he stood to his feet, gave Russo the finger, and then grabbed at his crotch in one quick motion.

"Very cute, Menace. We'll see who's gonna be the one getting fucked next Friday in court," Detective Russo laughed.

The detective sat back in his seat and rolled up his window as his partner drove off slowly.

"Man. I wish I knew where that cracker stayed," Menace said out loud as he watched the

Crown Vic go down the block. He slammed his fist in his other hand wishing it was Russo's face.

"Yo, that's that pig that G Money's been selling crack to," Lucky said between pulls.

Everybody turned their attention to Lucky. A smile spread across Menace's face as an idea popped into his head.

* * *

"That the house right there," Lucky pointed from the backseat of an old run-down station wagon they had rented from a trusted fiend.

Speedy, Menace, Lil Man, and Lucky all sat in the middle of the block across from a shotgun house.

"That old place?" Speedy asked.

He looked at the shutters barely holding on by a limb on the windows. It didn't look fit for a homeless person, much less a spot to hustle out of.

"That's the place," Lucky confirmed before looking up the block. "As a matter of fact, that's the nigger G right there."

They all focused their attention on the kid walking up the block toward them. They watched the kid struggle with the bags of groceries in his arms. He almost dropped them twice trying to find the right key to open the front door.

G Money was a short and stocky dark-skin kid with braids. From his flashy jewelry, crisp new outfit, and the brand new Js he wore, anyone could tell he was getting money. Word around town was that G Money caught a charge a year ago and Detective Russo was the arresting officer. Russo would come around and extort G Money for his dope to trick with a few of the local fiends or when he wanted to get lifted himself. In exchange, G Money kept his freedom.

The crew sat patiently as a female customer made her way up to the house once he finally got the door open. Once they were in the house, Speedy and the boys hopped out of the car and made their move. Speedy and Lil Man took up the front while Menace and Lucky went to the back, just in case G Money tried to make a run for it.

After the fiend got what she had come for, she opened the door to make her exit. Fear instantly came over her as she stared down the barrel of Speedy's .45.

"Shhhhh, don't make a sound," Speedy warned as he pushed her back into the house.

"What the fuck you want now, bitch? I told you I ain't giving you no more sh—"

Before he could finish cursing her out, G Money saw Speedy and Lil Man standing in the middle of the front room. He quickly turned on his heels and fled toward the back door in an attempt at a clean getaway.

"Shit," G Money shouted, when he opened the back door and was struck by the butt of Menace's Ruger P89.

"The shit is in the freezer," G pointed as blood from the deep gash above his left brow flowed into his eye.

He knew the routine all too well.

"Damn! Why couldn't it have been this easy when I was stickin' up niggas?" Speedy thought to himself as he entered the back room.

"Hey, Lucky, go in the front with Lil Man and

help keep an eye on shorty," Menace instructed.

Lucky nodded and did as he was told. Once he was out of the room Menace began with the questions.

"We're gonna make this sweet and simple. We want Russo," Menace admitted as he bent down in G Money's face.

While Menace waited for an answer, Speedy went to the freezer and emptied it of the stash that was inside.

"Russo," G Money asked, confused. "That's what this is all about? Shit, y'all didn't have to do all this. I would've gladly gave y'all the 411 on that pig," he assured them as he stood to his feet.

For the next fifteen minutes G Money told them about everything, including Russo's two daughters, where he lived, and the name of the chick he tricked with on occasions. By the time G Money was finished talking, they even knew the name of Russo's dog.

After they were satisfied, Speedy and Menace dragged G Money in to the living room, where Lil

Man and Lucky had the fiend gagged and bound in the middle of the floor.

"We good," Speedy told the youngsters as he stepped over the fiend and made his way to the front door.

"What's up?" Menace asked when he saw Lil Man and Lucky still standing in the same spot.

Without responding, Lucky turned the fiend over and looked her in her eyes before he put a bullet between them. G Money knew what time it was and started toward the back door before he got gunned down by Lil Man. G Money let out a blood-curdling scream as all three shots found a home in his back. Speedy and Menace couldn't believe that the two youngsters really had the heart to kill in a blink of an eye.

"Now that's gangsta!" Speedy replied as they made their way out the door and back to the hood.

When they finally made it back to the spot, Speedy and Menace weighed out the work that they took from G Money's freezer. It came up to a little over nine ounces of powder. Without any hesitation, they gave it all to Lil Man and Lucky for the work they put in. It was a small token of appreciation they wanted to give to them for showing they were down for the cause.

* * *

"You sure he got off at midnight?" Menace asked Speedy.

They looked at the clock on the dashboard of the stolen Chevy Impala that read 12:45 a.m. Menace's patience was wearing thinner and thinner as each minute went by.

"Yeah, that's what that lil nigga G Money told us," Speedy replied, glancing across the street at the address on the mailbox in front of the house.

"That looks like him coming up the street now," Speedy announced in a whisper.

They both slouched down in their seats as a set of headlights approached from the rear.

"Yup, that's that pig," Menace confirmed.

They both watched as Russo pulled his Crown Vic into his driveway. They sat back up when they heard Russo kill the engine. They watched him light up a cigarette before he called it a night.

"Perfect," Menace thought to himself as he pulled down the ski mask on his head over his face as Speedy did the same.

Running across the street with guns in hand, Speedy and Menace never would have guessed in a million years what their eyes saw once they drew down on Russo.

"What the—?" Russo shouted as he dropped the stem full of crack to the floor.

He reached for his service revolver, but it was too late. The first bullet ripped through Russo's head, and the following slugs rested in his upper body. After emptying their entire clips, they left the same way they came—unnoticed. It was lucky that the silencers that they had on their guns kept the noise down to a minimum. They laughed as they got on Highway 91 and headed back to the east side of town.

"I guess you won't be taking that trip upstate after all," Speedy joked as he glanced over at his partner.

Menace took out the blunt they were smoking on before they reached Russo's place and re-lit it.

"I know that's right," Menace agreed with a smile on his face. "I guess I got the last laugh, pig," he said out loud to the deceased detective. "I wish the youngsters could be here with us right now," Menace admitted as his thoughts drifted off to his little brother, Tommy.

* * *

"Yo! Don't have me out there waiting on your stupid ass all day neither," Menace barked at the caller on the other end of the phone.

"Come on, dawg. Don't even try to play me like that," J.B. laughed before Menace hung up the phone in his ear.

Menace hated serving J.B., mainly because J.B. lived on the north side of town where he had beef with a couple guys, and he knew if he got caught slipping in their territory, it would be his ass.

After Menace weighed out the four and a half ounces J.B. ordered, he checked his clip, tucked his nina in his waistline, and headed down the stairs to the front door.

"Hey, Ma. If anybody calls or comes by looking for me, tell 'em I'll be back in about an hour," Menace told his mother, Ms. Louis, as he retrieved his jacket from the coat rack beside the front door.

"Where you going?" Ms. Louis asked, never taking her eyes from the television set.

Little Tommy sat up with a big smile on his face as he listened to the conversation between his mother and big brother.

"I'm about to go to the store," Menace replied, once he had his jacket on.

That was all Little Tommy needed to hear.

"I wanna go," Little Tommy screamed, always jumping at the opportunity to hang with his older brother.

Little Tommy was a thirteen-year-old version of his big brother, Menace. He was tall and lanky, and he had gray eyes and curly hair. He worshiped the ground his brother walked on, and he wanted to be just like him when he grew up. Menace loved his brother just as much and showed it by spoiling him to no end, so Tommy wouldn't resort to the streets as he did coming up. Whatever Tommy wanted, all he had to do was let his big brother know—and that's exactly what he did.

Menace paused for a second as Tommy ran out of the living room and snatched his coat off the coat rack. He stared at Menace with hopeful eyes as he slid into it, waiting for Menace to say it was okay. But before he could say anything, Ms. Louis spoke up. "Go ahead and spend some quality time with your little brother before you hit them streets.

Menace took off his hat and put it on Tommy's head, and then slapped the brim. Little Tommy grinned from ear to ear and followed his brother's footsteps to the car.

"As soon as I make this run, I'ma take you to the mall and buy you an outfit and a new pair of Js for making the honor roll," Menace told his brother as he started the engine to his new Benz and pulled away from the curb.

"Yo, this ride is hot!" Tommy admitted as he stuck his arm out the window. "When I grow up, I wanna be just like you, Menace."

Menace took his eyes off the road and glanced over at his little brother as he stared out of the window at a group of girls dressed in Daisy Dukes and halter tops, trying to beat the summer's heat. Tommy felt like the man as the young girls smiled and waved at them as they passed them by.

"Nah, lil' bruh. You gonna be better than I am. That's why I push you so hard and reward you for doing good in school. If you don't remember nothing else I have taught you, I want you to remember education comes first."

Tommy listened to the jewels his big brother was dropping on him and nodded his head in understanding.

"Then you get the money and the bitches," Menace joked as he put his hand on top of Tommy's head and shook it.

* * *

"Yo! Where you at?" Menace yelled into the phone at J.B.

He had been sitting in front of Finch Street Park

for over ten minutes now waiting on him to show up. He instantly regretted not having J.B. come to his side of town. He felt like a sitting duck waiting to be killed.

"I'm right around the corner. I'll be there in less than a minute," J.B. claimed as Menace ended the call in frustration.

He then checked his surroundings for anything out of the ordinary. Two minutes later Menace noticed J.B.'s old Toyota Corolla come smoking around the corner. As much money as J.B. should have been making, Menace couldn't understand for the life of him why he wouldn't invest a few grand in a new whip.

"Sit tight. I'll be right back," Menace told Little Tommy as he got out of his car to meet J.B. in the park.

The park was rather empty for a Saturday evening. That was good for Menace. That meant there wouldn't be many prying eyes in his business. He also could keep his eyes open for anyone who looked suspicious.

"My fault, homie. I had to drop my baby mama off at the beauty salon," J.B. apologized as he went into his pocket and pulled out the money for the pack.

After making sure all $3,200 was there, Menace went into one of his cargo pockets and pulled out a big ziplock bag filled with the work. Menace watched J.B. get into his car and pull off before he made his way to his. As soon as he reached for the door handle, a strange feeling came over him that made him glance at the corner, where he noticed a dark blue, four-door hooptie creeping his way. Just as he put his hand on his 9mm, bullets began to ring out. Menace quickly jumped over the hood of his Benz and took cover before he returned fire. The small shootout only lasted a few seconds, but to the few pedestrians at the park, it seemed to last a lifetime as they scattered for shelter from the rapid gunfire from Menace's loud cannon and the semiautomatic weapons from the hooptie.

Once the shots ceased, Menace stood to his feet and looked around into the park. He saw a little girl, no older than six years old, laid out in the middle of the merry-go-round in a puddle of blood.

"Damn!" he cursed himself as he turned to check on Little Tommy.

When he opened the passenger side door, all he could do was stare in disbelief as his only brother took his last breath and closed his eyes.

THE NEXT MORNING

"This is Arnessia Williams reporting live from outside of Detective Joey Russo's home, where he was gunned down in cold blood in his police car. No suspects have been identified, but from the drugs found on his person and in his care, this has been labeled a drug-related murder. More news to come at noon. Thank you for tuning in to WCLS Channel 11 News. Back to you, Jack."

***

First thing Monday morning, Menace's lawyer contacted him with the good news that his case was being dismissed due to the death of their star witness, and the recording they had of the sell had inadvertently gotten recorded over. In layman's terms, they had no evidence. That was music to Menace's ears as he smiled and lay back as Crystal gave him the blow job of a lifetime.

* * *

Early Friday morning, Speedy received a text message from Tawana asking him to meet her at Applebee's for lunch. He was reluctant to meet her at first, but he agreed to anyway.

He arrived first and sat at the table, with a thousand thoughts running through his head. On several occasions, he thought about up and leaving, but forced himself to stay. Twenty minutes later, he watched as she entered the restaurant. He was surprised at how much her belly had grown over the past few months. The crazy thing of it all was that he didn't even know how many months she was. As she waddled her way over to the table, Speedy's heart softened. No matter how mad he may have been before seeing her, it didn't seem to matter at that time. He couldn't deny the love he felt for her.

He stood to his feet with a smile on his face and pulled her chair out for her.

"Thank you," she smiled as she took her seat across from him.

"So how have you been?" Speedy asked once he sat himself in front of her.

Her smile slowly faded as she responded, "I've been good." She looked him in his eyes and placed her right hand over her stomach.

Guilt instantly took over as Speedy glanced down at the table and broke their eye contact.

"That's good," he replied as he waved over the waitress so they could place their order. "I guess I deserved that," Speedy admitted as the waitress walked over.

Once they ordered, an awkward silence fell upon them.

"So, what are you having?" he asked, breaking the silence.

Tawana looked at him and then rolled her eyes.

"We're having a son," she replied, clearly irritated.

Her attitude was making it very hard for him to remain cool.

"Oh, are we?" Speedy snapped with a hint of doubt in his tone.

Even though he didn't ask the question to hurt her, he wanted to know the truth. There wasn't a day that went by since the night he left and she told him she was pregnant, that he didn't wonder if she got pregnant by him or not. Truth be told, Tawana didn't honestly know who the father was herself, even though she prayed to God each and every night that it turned out to be Speedy's.

She knew how badly Speedy wanted a son, and she found out earlier that day that she was having a boy. She couldn't bring herself to tell him that it was his when there was a slight chance that it wasn't, so she gave him the only answer she could. "I don't know, Marcus," she replied with tears in her eyes.

Speedy stood to his feet as the muscles in his jaws tightened and his fists clenched. He pulled out a $100 bill, placed it on the table, and then turned to head toward the door.

"I love you, Marcus," Tawana said in a whisper.

She then hung her head to the floor, no longer able to hold up her tough girl composure. Speedy's heart dropped to the pit of his stomach as he turned around and looked down at her.

"I wish you would've thought about that before you fucked him," Speedy harshly stated in a low but calm tone.

All that ran through his mind was how she had betrayed him, before he turned back around and made his way out of the restaurant, leaving her to drown in her own misery.

* * *

Menace was sitting on the steps of his apartment building smoking a blunt when Speedy pulled up to his complex.

"So how did things go between you and Tawana at lunch?" Menace asked, and then standing to his feet to greet his partner.

After their short embrace, Menace passed the blunt to him. He could tell the situation was weighing heavy on his mind due to the stress lines in his forehead.

"Man, she don't even know if I'm the father or not," Speedy revealed as he took a seat and took a long pull of the blunt to relieve the pain.

Menace ran his hands the length of his face and shook his head in disbelief. Not even he could think of words to say to ease the pain that he knew his partner was feeling. Menace listened as Speedy carried on and on, venting his feelings.

"Then the bitch had the nerve to say that she loves me."

Speedy took another hit and then passed the blunt back to Menace, which he readily accepted.

"The nerve of that bitch!" Speedy said.

Not really knowing what to say, Menace just took in the smoke and then exhaled. "Yo! That's some deep shit!" Menace admitted. "To tell you the truth, you're one hell of a nigga, because I know if I was in your shoes, ain't no telling what I would've done to the bitch after I would've killed the nigga!" Menace fumed as he bit down on his bottom lip. "My bad, dawg," he apologized, after he realized that he had called Tawana out of her name.

"You good, my nigga. But to tell you the truth, if it wasn't for Fuzzy being here for me, I probably would've done some stupid-ass shit," Speedy admitted as he took the awaiting blunt. "She really helped a nigga get through this for real."

Speedy sat back and thought about all of the long nights when he was unable to sleep and Fuzzy comforted him by holding him in her arms and giving him advice. Not once did she talk down on Tawana to get closer to him, and that's what he admired about her. The more time they spent together, the easier it was for him to move on. She even promised that if the baby turned out to be his, she would be there for him to help take care of the kid. That in itself said a lot about her.

"Oh, I didn't know you were out here, Speedy," Crystal claimed, when she opened the door and stuck out her head. She looked over at Menace and informed him that dinner was ready.

"All right. Give me a few minutes, and I'll be in there," Menace promised.

Crystal looked at Speedy before turning around and heading back into the apartment. "You're welcome to join us," she shouted over her shoulder before disappearing into the apartment.

Once the door was closed, Speedy spoke on the real reason he stopped by in the first place. "Before I forget, I got some information on that nigga King from the north side of town," Speedy began as he rose to his feet.

"King . . . King . . . King . . ." Menace repeated to no one in particular as he tried to put a face with the name. "You talking 'bout that nigga with the candy-apple-red Bentley GT who owns The King's Palace night club?" Menace asked, remembering the flamboyant hustler that also ran the entire north side of the city's drug trade market.

King was a well-known, respected, and not to mention feared kingpin in Wilson. He stood about six foot four with a muscular build to match. What set him apart from the rest was that he wasn't only street smart, but he was book smart as well. He chose to follow in the footsteps of his father-in-law after he was killed, and he hadn't looked back since.

"That's the one," Speedy verified. "You down to make this come-up, or what?"

Menace looked at Speedy as if he was crazy. "You know it." Menace rubbed his hands together in anticipation of the money they were sure to make off the lick.

"Your food is getting cold," Crystal impatiently yelled from the other side of the door, interrupting their scheme.

After agreeing to meet up at the spot later on, Speedy made his way to his car. He had big plans on his mind as he headed out of the parking lot. As soon as he turned onto the empty street, the first person he saw was Tawana. She passed by him on her way to Crystal's apartment. Their eyes locked, but neither of them acknowledged the other. Speedy wanted to turn around, but he decided against it. Instead, he sped down the block, turned up his radio, and jumped on the highway and headed home to be with his queen.

10

For the next couple of weeks, Speedy and Menace kept a close eye on the notorious King. They realized it wouldn't be as easy as they thought it was going to be to get at him, because he wasn't the average type of hustler. He stayed with goons by his side wherever he went, and they would lay down their lives to protect his. Not to mention, he changed up his routine and cars daily. The only thing that remained the same was there was someone driving his Bentley GT to pick him up every Saturday night after visiting the club. Due to the limo-black tint, it was difficult to see who was driving inside. Another problem they had was the location where his house was located. It was so far outside the city limits that he would've known from the jump if he was being followed.

They finally decided to call it a night after another useless evening of surveillance. Little did they know they were being watched as well.

* * *

"I'm in the guestroom," Fuzzy called out from upstairs as Speedy entered the house.

He couldn't wait to get upstairs to steal a kiss from the love of his life. No matter how bad his day may have been, having Fuzzy in his arms always seemed to boost his soul.

"What you doin' in—?" Speedy questioned as he walked through the doorway of the guestroom, but stopped mid-sentence when he looked around the room. "What's all this?" he asked with outstretched arms, pointing at the many baby gifts scattered all about.

Fuzzy slowly made her way over to Speedy with her arms hidden behind her back. He tried his best to sneak a peek, but Fuzzy wouldn't allow him.

"Close your eyes," she demanded, backing up to the wall.

Once Speedy did as he was told, she walked back up to him and told him to open them. He looked at the positive sign on the pregnancy test that

Fuzzy held in front of his face.

"You're going to be a daddy," she verified.

"Are you serious?" Speedy asked as he grabbed her by the waist, lifted her up, and spun her around.

"Yes, baby," Fuzzy dizzily replied once he sat her back down on her feet.

Fuzzy put both hands on the sides of her head and tried to stop the room from spinning. She then placed them on the side of Speedy's face and planted a kiss on his lips.

No more words were exchanged as Speedy carried her across the hall to their bedroom where they made love all through the night and into the early hours of the morning.

* * *

Speedy got up early and snuck out of the room to surprise Fuzzy with a romantic breakfast in bed. He tiptoed into the kitchen and rummaged through the fridge looking for ingredients to prepare a decent meal for his new baby mama. He wanted to fix something special, so he bypassed the milk and cereal and grabbed a crate of eggs, a can of buttermilk biscuits, a pack of turkey bacon, and a carton of orange juice. After walking over to the cabinet to retrieve the box of grits, he was ready to start the task at hand.

An hour and an entire crate of eggs later, Speedy's mission was complete. Before walking out of the kitchen, he cleaned up his mess and threw away the batteries he took out of the smoke detector.

"Awww," Fuzzy smiled as Speedy entered the bedroom with a platter full of breakfast.

He returned the smile once he saw the joy in her eyes. When he got to the bed, he placed the platter on her lap. She burst into laughter when she saw the lumpy grits, runny eggs, and the two crisp biscuits.

"Bae, I know you meant well and all . . . and . . . and it really is the thought that counts and all, but—!" Speedy looked down on the plate and picked up a piece of bacon.

"I thought we agreed to not judge a book by its cover," Speedy reminded her, before biting into the piece of bacon.

"Your car or mine?" Fuzzy asked as she looked

at the bitter expression Speedy held on his face.

"Yours," he replied once he spit the burnt bacon back onto the platter and wiped his mouth.

They both laughed as Speedy took the tray back into the kitchen while Fuzzy made her way into the bathroom to take a shower.

Speedy and Fuzzy shared breakfast at the Waffle House off of Highway 264 and I-95 before he offered to take her shopping. She quickly declined, but after Speedy's insistence, Fuzzy gave in and they made their way to Triangle Mall in Raleigh.

Once he came out of the second store with Fuzzy several hours later, Speedy decided to sit out the next few stores.

"I'll be in the lobby area," he informed her, after shoving a wad of bills into her handbag.

Before she could refuse, Speedy turned around and walked off, leaving her standing there shaking her head and smiling.

"Damn! I'm glad I gave him a chance," she thought to herself as she watched him round the corner.

She turned and made her way into Macy's—her favorite store. Fuzzy spent an hour there and then made her way to Lord & Taylor's, where a cute off-white Vera Wang dress instantly caught her attention as she walked by the maternity department.

"I got to have this," she thought as she snatched it off the rack and rushed to the fitting room to try it on.

She hated to keep Speedy waiting because she knew how impatient men could be when they weren't shopping with their woman, so she wanted to be as quick as she possibly could.

Since Fuzzy had the dress on, she stepped out to take a good look at herself in the full-length mirror outside of the fitting room. She admired the way the dress caressed the midsection of her slightly plump belly. She smiled before she spun on her heels feeling like Cinderella on ball night. When she came to a complete stop to get one final look before purchasing it, her heart skipped a beat.

"What are you doing here?" she asked surprised as a single tear built up in her eye.

"The same reason everyone else is in here," Donte replied, eyeing up Fuzzy from behind. "I see you've been taking care of yourself," he complimented as he tapped her on the ass lightly.

Fuzzy turned around and pushed him in the chest before she knew it. "Don't touch me, Donte," she warned, no longer able to hold in the tears in.

Donte threw his hands up in the air and took a step back. He glanced down, and for the first time, he noticed she was pregnant.

"Oh, that's the reason your ass and hips are poking out like that," Donte said, placing his pointer finger and thumb up under his chin.

"Pffff! Whatever, Donte." Fuzzy waved him off. "Don't you have some low-income hood-rat chick to harass or something?"

She turned around and made her way back into the fitting room to put her clothes back on without waiting for a response.

"Nope. I'm trying to take my wife out to lunch

and catch up on old times," he replied, checking himself out in the mirror.

Fuzzy shook her head and listened to Donte run his game. She couldn't believe he had the nerve to come at her the way he was after all he had put her through. She wanted to change clothes before she said or did something she might regret in the future, but the hood in her wouldn't allow him to get off the hook that easy.

"Your who? Don't even play yourself like that, Donte! What we shared is over, dead, gone. It's reached its end. The sooner you realize that fact, the better both of our lives will be."

Fuzzy stormed out of the fitting room with the dress thrown over her right arm.

"Ummm, is that right?" Donte asked, blocking Fuzzy from making her exit.

She stood face to face with the man she once loved, but now with hate in her eyes.

"You'll never find another man who will do for you the things I have," Donte boasted with confidence.

"You just don't get it, do you?" Fuzzy asked, before she shook her head, walked around him, and made her way to the register.

Before the clerk rang up her purchase, she turned to face Donte once again.

"Oh yeah? By the way, my new man is more of a man than you ever have been!" she admitted, with a smile on her face.

"And in bed?"

Fuzzy bit down on her bottom lip and then closed her eyes. When she opened them and looked into Donte's face, the sight was priceless. After paying for her dress, she stormed out of the department store to find her man. She just hoped that Donte wouldn't follow her to make things worse.

"You ready?" Speedy asked as he watched Fuzzy march in his direction with a drained look on her face.

"Yeah," she replied dryly.

She walked up and planted a kiss on his lips. She handed her bags to Speedy, and then led the way to the mall's exit door.

They were both lost in their own thoughts as they walked through the parking lot on the way to Fuzzy's car. Speedy was loading the bags into the trunk when he heard a male's voice speak up from behind him.

"I'll see you later, Fuzzy," Donte called out from the passenger side of his Escalade.

Speedy turned around, and in one swift motion, he had his gun aimed at the middle of Donte's forehead.

"Whoaaaa, cowboy. I wouldn't do that if I was you!" Donte warned.

All of the windows on the Escalade rolled down, and several goons with assault rifles appeared from them. The fact that Speedy was outnumbered and outgunned didn't matter to him. The only thing that stopped him from putting a hole in the middle of Donte's head was Fuzzy and his unborn seed resting in her stomach.

"No," Fuzzy screamed as she stood in front of Speedy with her arms outstretched.

Speedy tried moving Fuzzy out of the way without taking his eyes off of Donte.

"I'll see you around, playboy," Donte threatened, then motioned for his goons to put their weapons away.

Yeah. Sooner than you think! Speedy thought to himself as he watched Donte's Escalade drive off.

* * *

"Why in the hell didn't you tell me you were married to that nigga King?" Speedy asked, pacing back and forth in their bedroom.

Fuzzy sat at the foot of their bed and watched as Speedy blew off some steam.

"Speedy, I told you I was once married to Donte," she reminded him. "I told you everything the night you stayed at my apartment, remember?"

Speedy stopped in front of her and tried to control his breathing.

"Fuzzy, you told me about some nigga named Donte, not that nigga King!" Speedy shouted angrily.

He walked over to the closet door and punched

a hole in it. Fuzzy stood to her feet and walked over to Speedy and wrapped her arms around him from behind. She knew the reason Speedy was feeling that way.

"Baby, you have nothing to be worried about," she promised before she kissed the back of his neck. "It's you and me now."

Speedy turned to face her and saw the sincerity in her eyes. After kissing her lips, Fuzzy looked down at the floor.

"Baby, there's more."

Fuzzy grabbed him by the hand and led him to the bed. There she explained how Donte used to work for her father before he got killed, and now he worked for her uncle. After assuring Speedy that her dealings with Donte were over after they divorced, her cell phone began to ring.

"Hello. Yes, fine. No, sir. That's not necessary. Please don't. I promise. Okay. See you then. Bye. I love you."

Fuzzy ended the called and then looked into Speedy's eyes.

"My uncle wants to meet with you tomorrow."

"Yeah, whatever!" Speedy responded before walking out of the bedroom.

He headed to the living room, where he lay on the couch to get his thoughts together. He remembered Fuzzy telling him that her father was a major figure in the underworld, but he never would have imagined in a million years that her father was the legendary Mr. Biggs. As he dozed off to sleep he said a silent prayer that there would be no other unexpected secrets about her life that she had left out.

11

"*I couldn't sleep,*" *Fuzzy* whispered when Speedy opened his eyes and looked down at her lying on his chest.

He glanced over at the grandfather clock in the corner that read 11:00 a.m. He then cursed himself for sleeping in so late.

"Come on! Get up! We only got an hour to meet up with my uncle," she reminded him as she slid from under the covers and revealed her naked body on her way to the shower. Speedy watched her perfectly round ass until she was out of sight.

"Damn! Her uncle must be that nigga!" Speedy thought to himself as they pulled up in the parking lot of Big Mama's Kitchen and an all-black Rolls-Royce parked in front of the establishment.

Fuzzy parked behind her uncle's car and took a deep breath before killing the engine.

"You nervous?" she asked once they got out of

the car and headed into the restaurant.

"Should I be?" he asked as he held open the door for her to enter.

Before she walked in, she gave Speedy an assuring look.

"Of course not, sweety." She winked, pinched the dimple on his left cheek, and then strutted her way inside.

Speedy shook his head and followed behind her, watching her ass the entire time.

When Speedy looked up, he noticed the restaurant was empty, besides a dark-skinned man sitting at a table in the very back with two bearish-looking men standing on each side of him.

"Uncle Slim," Fuzzy called out with outstretched arms as she made her way over to the table to greet him.

Slim was exactly what he was—a tall, lanky, frail-looking man with cold eyes. He wore a neck, wrist, and hand full of gold that showed off his ranks in the underworld. He was loved in his community but feared throughout the city. All in all, he was respected by everyone with whom he came in contact.

Slim smiled, put out his cigar, and stood to his feet when he noticed his niece coming his way.

"Look at you! You look like you're about to pop," he joked, before he then embraced Fuzzy and planted a single kiss on each one of her cheeks.

Fuzzy blushed, glanced at Speedy, and cleared her throat.

"This is my fiancé, Marcus," she introduced, intertwining her arms in his.

Speedy began to extend his arm out to shake Slim's hand, but before he could fully extend it Slim's two bodyguards intervened. Speedy was quickly patted down and relieved of the Glock .40 he had concealed in his waistline.

"Excuse us, Chantel," Slim ordered without taking his eyes off of Speedy.

Fuzzy looked to her uncle and then back to Speedy.

"I'll be in the back," she whispered, before walking out.

Speedy watched her leave the room. So many thoughts flashed through his head, including why

Slim wanted to meet with him.

"Have a seat," Slim demanded as he took his seat and re-lit the cigar he had in his hand.

He inhaled the smoke from the expensive cigar, and then exhaled it in the air.

"Straight from Cuba," Slim admitted, before he reached inside his tailor-made Armani suit jacket to offer one to Speedy.

"Not to be rude, sir, but why did you want to meet with me?" Speedy asked, not wanting to beat around the bush any longer.

"Straight to the point. That's what I like."

Slim dipped his cigar in the ashtray and put it out once again. Before answering, Slim snapped his fingers twice, and a waitress appeared out of nowhere and filled his glass back up to the top. When she finished, she made her way back out of sight.

"I wanted to meet the man my niece has been spending her time with," Slim began as he looked Speedy in his eyes. "You know, to see if you're capable of protecting her if need be."

Slim studied the young man in front of him

before continuing.

"You see, I've had my people do a little investigation on you."

Slim's last statement caught Speedy totally by surprise.

"Oh, you did, huh? And what did they come up with?"

Speedy didn't like the fact that Slim knew about him while he knew nothing of him. Slim propped his elbows on the table and leaned forward slowly.

"Let's just say I know you and your crew are more than able to handle any problem that comes your way."

A smile of confidence spread across Speedy's face after hearing his response.

"But what I'm really concerned about is if you are able to take care of her financially."

Speedy thought about the $100,000 that he had put up for a rainy day and felt like that was more than enough for him and Fuzzy to live off of comfortably.

"Of course, I am," Speedy boasted, and arrogantly leaned back in his seat.

"Very well then," Slim shouted with satisfaction before he clapped his hands together.

"Let's get down to business."

Those were the words Speedy had been waiting to hear for years.

"How much work do you and your crew move?" Slim asked as he rubbed his hands together.

Speedy looked up at the ceiling and began calculating the amount in his head.

"About two or three bricks," he replied.

"And how long does it take for you to get rid of the kilos?"

Even though Speedy already knew the answer to the question, he paused before he responded.

"I say about a week."

Slim sat back in silence to see if he could tell if Speedy was serious or not.

"You're good!" Slim shouted out, before he let out a historical laugh. His bodyguards joined in as he slammed his palms against the table. "You almost had me going there, kid. Did y'all hear this guy?"

The two bodyguards nodded their heads in

agreement and continued to laugh.

"Look here, Marcus," Slim announced as he stopped laughing and became serious in a blink of an eye.

"I'm going to front you ten kilos of pure cocaine on consignment. Can you handle that?"

Speedy sat up in his seat and looked Slim in his eyes. He felt like everybody in the room could hear his heart beating in his chest as he thought of the right words to say. In no way did he want to blow the proposition in front of him.

"No doubt," he responded with confidence. "And by the way, please call me Speedy," he clarified for future reference.

Slim nodded his head in understanding.

"Good. Tomorrow I want you to come here at twelve noon. There will be a late-model pickup truck in the parking lot with the keys in the ignition. The kilos will be buried in the equipment in the back of it," Slim instructed.

"Once you finish that, get back at me, and we'll go from there."

On one hand Speedy was happy to be connected,

but on the other hand he hoped he hadn't bitten off more than he could chew.

It's do or die, Speedy thought to himself as he sealed the deal.

"I'll be here."

Slim stood to his feet, wiped off his jacket, and then made his way to the door. Before he made his exit, Slim snapped his fingers and one of the bodyguards turned around and set Speedy's gun on the podium beside the door. After Slim walked out, Fuzzy made her way back into the room, breaking him out of his thoughts.

"Is everything okay?"

Speedy looked in her direction before he replied.

"Things couldn't be better!" he assured her as he stood to his feet. "Let's get out of here."

As they made their way to the door, Speedy stopped at the podium and retrieved his gun. But something nagged at Speedy's gut since he entered the restaurant, so he asked.

"Does the owner know him or something?"

Fuzzy looked around at the empty establishment before she replied, "Of course I know him."

She blew him a kiss, walked out of Big Mama's, and headed to her car. Speedy stood there speechless for a second as he took in what Fuzzy had just said.

"You bullshitting?" he called out as he tucked his gun back into its rightful place and then jogged outside behind her.

He thought back to the first date they had, and laughed to himself when he remembered how she insisted on paying the bill. Speedy glanced over the roof of the car at Fuzzy before they got inside.

"I know you're thinking, so to clarify things, let me tell you. I did actually pay for our meal," Fuzzy said.

Speedy laughed once he opened his door, before he got in and yelled out, "Yeah right!"

Fuzzy laughed as she lowered herself behind the wheel and started the car.

"For real," she admitted as she slid on her shades, put her car in drive, and drove out into traffic.

12

The following day Speedy got Menace to take him by Big Mama's Kitchen to pick up the truck with the work in it. Just as promised, the truck was in the exact spot Slim said it would be. Speedy got out of Menace's Benz and looked around before opening up the pickup truck's door.

"Bingo!" he said to himself when he saw the key hanging from the ignition.

Speedy led the way back to the spot with big plans for the future.

After they unloaded the truck, Speedy and Menace spent the rest of the afternoon watching Shelia whip it up. For her, turning the ten kilos of cocaine into fifteen kilos of crack was the easiest task she ever performed. They all sat for hours and bagged up rocks ranging from nics to dimes to twenties, and all the way up to ounces for their small-time hustlers. They had ziplock bags for their clients that wanted big eights or better. Once they had everything bagged up and ready for distribution, Speedy and Menace called over Lil Man and Lucky.

Lil Man and Lucky now had new jobs to fulfill as recruiters for the new team Speedy and Menace were trying to build. The move was successful. Within a couple of weeks, they had a squad of young, ambitious hustlers backing them, not to mention a few real-life killers. With their help, the fifteen kilos a week quickly grew to thirty kilos, and they were able to lock down the entire east side of the city in no time.

* * *

Speedy lay back in the passenger's seat on his cell phone while Menace cruised the streets in his new mint-green S-type Jag.

"That's what's up. I'm on my way over there now," Speedy ended his call with a big smile on his face.

"What the fuck are you so happy about over there?" Menace asked as he looked at his partner.

"I need you to run me by Richie's Cycle Center right quick," he replied before digging in his pocket and pulling out a wad of cash.

Menace didn't bother to ask any more questions when he found out where Speedy needed to go. All Menace had on his mind was how he was going to convince Shon to go out on a date with him. After making a right onto Goldsboro Street, he pulled into the opening between the fence that surrounded the shop.

"Damn! That bitch looks good," Speedy admitted once he set his eyes on the stretched out, flat, black 2005 Suzuki 1000 with the big-boy kit on the back tire that Shon stood beside.

"You ain't never lied," Menace agreed without even looking at the motorcycle.

As soon as they stepped out of the car, Menace went straight into attack mode.

"What's good, baby? You about ready to go out on that date?"

Menace licked his lips and stared at Shon like a piece of meat.

"Oh Lord. Speedy, get your boy," Shon laughed while she shook her head from side to side. "Why didn't you tell me you had him with you?"

Speedy burst out in laughter as he walked up on the two.

Shon was a short, attractive, around-the-way girl who put you in the mind of the old school female rapper MC Lyte. She was known around Wilson and the surrounding areas for her skills on two wheels as well as surrounding herself with a beautiful stable of women she kept by her side at all times. That was one of the main reasons she never gave Menace any play on his numerous advances.

"Now, now, now, you kids! Y'all play nice, sis!" Speedy joked as he walked up on her and gave her a hug.

Throughout their years of doing business, Speedy and Shon became close and referred to each other as brother and sister. After their short embrace, Shon backed up and handed him the keys to the bike.

"You wanna take it for a spin to see how she rides?"

"Do you wanna count the money?" Speedy smirked, feeling a little insulted as he handed her the $10,000.

"Nope," she replied when she took the money, put it in her back pocket, and headed into the shop.

"I wouldn't mind riding that," Menace stated out loud, just as Shon grabbed the door handle.

"I'm sure you would!" Shon shot back before she disappeared into the shop.

"You know that offer still stands," he shouted after her. "Man! I gotta have her," he said to himself as he turned around and watched Speedy slide the helmet over his head.

"Keep on dreamin'," Speedy laughed as he jumped on his new bike and started the engine.

As soon as he put it in first gear, Shon stuck her head out the door and flagged him down before he pulled away.

"I almost forgot to let you know, when you hold it at full throttle for three seconds straight, NOS automatically shoots to the motor," she warned.

Speedy grinned, slammed the shield down over his face, and revved up the motor. The sound of the motor sent chills down his spine as he pulled into the middle of the street and put the RPMs at 6,500. When he released the clutch, everything seemed to go by in a blur. Shon shook her head and laughed, and then she made her way back into the shop before the smoke from the tire cleared the air.

Later on that day when Lil Man and Lucky came to the spot, they were greeted with gifts. Speedy and Menace felt that it was only right to reward the two that made it all possible for them to climb the ladder of success so fast.

"This is what I'm talking about," Lil Man shouted as he walked around the new pearl-white Lincoln LS.

It was parked right in front of Lucky's money-green Monte Carlo SS.

"I'ma get plenty of bitches in this," Lucky boasted as he jumped in the front seat and started up the engine.

He couldn't wait to put a set of shoes on it.

"I'ma call this muthafucka the Incredible Hulk!"

The crew burst into laughter, and then decided to bend a few corners to show off their new toys.

13

Speedy and Menace felt like they had finally built up their weight in the game. Their names were ringing bells not only on the east side of the city, but also throughout the west and north sides. Speedy was sure that their names also rang in King's ears. That was the main reason he invited his entire crew out for a night on the town at The King's Palace.

The first thing they noticed when they pulled up to The King's Palace was the long line that wrapped around the building. One by one, they all exited their whips. All eyes were on them as they walked by the awaiting partygoers and headed straight to the front of the line. No one dared say a word, because they all knew of or had heard of who they were. After sliding the bouncers a grand to let them all in with their burners, they made their way to the VIP section of the club. They eyed the scantily dressed women as they walked by in next to nothing, trying to get their attention. If it was any other night they would have pursued the women, but they were on a mission this night.

"What do we got here?" King asked as he and his goons stood in front of Speedy and his crew's booth.

Speedy removed the bottle of Dom from his mouth, smiled, and then stood to his feet. No one knew how thick the tension in the room actually was, besides the two crews that now stood face to face.

"Let's take this to my office."

"After you," Speedy replied without ever breaking eye contact.

King and his goons led Speedy and his crew up the winding stairs to his office. Once they all entered, King took his seat behind the expensive cherry desk, and then he motioned for the crew to have a seat.

"We'd rather stand," Speedy let it be known before he placed his arms across his chest.

There was no way he was going to get caught slipping if King or his goons tried anything shysty.

"So, to what do I owe the pleasure?" King tried to keep his composure as he stared down the arrogant Speedy, who stood in front of him. "Making a pretty big name for yourselves since we last ran into each other," King admitted, running his hand over his neatly cut goatee. "It's like everywhere I turn I hear your name."

Speedy smirked, figuring King wanted in on his lucrative drug trade, now that he and his crew had made it a bit higher up the ladder. But there was no way in hell Speedy was going to get in bed with the enemy in any form or fashion, especially Chantel's ex-husband. However, what came out of King's mouth next totally took Speedy by surprise.

"All of that was cool, until I heard that you were making a few moves on the north side, and everyone knows that's strictly my turf!" King shouted and slammed his fist down against his desk. "And that makes you a thorn in my side."

King's threat angered Speedy and his crew. Before anything else was said, they all had their guns drawn. King's goons were ready for the beef and drew their guns as well. Silence filled the air as

Speedy and King waited patiently for the other to make the slightest movement that would indicate their well-being was in any further danger. Before giving the word, King saw the look in Speedy's eyes that let him know he was willing to die where he stood if the occasion caused for it.

"It's your call, playboy. How do you want to handle this?" Speedy asked.

He watched the sweat roll down King's forehead and onto his desk as he weighed out his options. Even though his crew's guns were bigger, King knew there was still a chance he could get killed in the act, so he did the most logical thing for the time being.

"Let 'em leave," King announced with a wave of his hand.

The goons lowered their weapons at his command and waited for further instructions. With weapons still drawn, Speedy's crew slowly backpedaled out of the office and into the hallway that led to the stairway. They didn't attempt to conceal their weapons until they opened the door that led back to the crowded club area. King looked at them from the two-way glass in his office until they made it out of the club.

"I want you to go down there and bring me the muthafucks that let them niggas in with their guns," King ordered with venom in his voice.

As soon as King's goon left his office, a smile spread across King's face.

"I can't wait to see the look across that arrogant face of yours when you finally connect the pieces to my little secret," King laughed as he walked over to the far wall and pulled down a sword.

THE NEXT MORNING

"Why are you up so early?" Fuzzy asked as she sat up behind Speedy and wrapped her arms around him.

She rubbed her breasts against his back and planted soft kisses on his neck. Since she became pregnant, her morning craving for sex was at an all-time high. Speedy was too focused on the television to fulfill her need at the time. When she glanced up to see what had his undivided attention, her mouth fell open.

"Good morning. This is Jasmine Moore reporting live from the back alley of the famous night club The King's Palace, where former bouncer Morris Hodges—AKA Big Moe's—body was found in a dumpster, with his head detached from the rest of his body. The local authorities are asking anyone with any leads to please call the crime stopper number at the bottom of your screen. All calls are confidential. We'll have more details at noon. This is Jasmine Moore signing out. Back to you, Bob."

Speedy turned off the television set, turned and faced his woman, and then looked in her eyes. He was expecting her to begin questioning him about his involvement in the crime that occurred last night, but she did not. Instead, she lay Speedy down on his back, kissed his stomach, and then took him into her mouth. All he could do was close his eyes and hold on for the ride as she sent him to ecstasy.

14

"Happy birthday," everyone screamed in unison once Fuzzy entered her restaurant.

She was totally taken by surprise, since she and Speedy met up there for lunch every Friday. Truth be told, she thought he had forgotten it was her birthday. She looked over at their table and saw her knight in shining armor waiting for her to join him.

"You shouldn't have, Speedy!" Fuzzy claimed as she approached the table.

Speedy greeted her with a hug and kiss, and then pulled out her chair for her.

"I thought you forgot," she admitted as he slid up her chair to the table and then sat down next to her.

"How could I? I still remember the threat you made when we first met if I ever forgot!" Speedy joked as he waved over the waiter.

"Here we go talking about the past. I told you I

was sorry, boy," Fuzzy laughed, thinking back to how she gave Speedy such a hard time when they first met.

"Your usual, sir?" Nicolas asked, with pad and pen in hand ready to take their order.

"That would be just fine," Fuzzy answered for them before Speedy could respond.

Nicolas nodded his head and turned to place the order to the kitchen.

"And bring your finest wine," Fuzzy called out to him over her shoulder before he got too far.

"Will do," Nicolas replied.

He retrieved the bottle of wine along with two champagne glasses, and then set them down on the table before going to put in their order.

Thirty minutes later, the waiter reappeared with their food on a silver platter. Once he set it in front of them, he made his way back to the kitchen.

"I want to make a toast," Speedy announced as he hit his fork on the side of the champagne glass.

Everyone stopped what they were doing and grabbed their glasses to join in on the toast.

"I want to give a toast to the birthday girl, who happens to be the most beautiful woman in the world to me."

All the women in the room oohed and aahed and put their hands over their hearts. Speedy looked over into Fuzzy's eyes before continuing.

"I made a promise to this woman when we first got together, that I would always love and protect her, and I have done exactly that, and in return, she's rewarded me by bearing my seed."

Fuzzy's eyes began to water as she listened to Speedy pour his heart out to her.

"And there's no other person in this universe I would rather share the rest of my life with than you."

Fuzzy put her hand over her mouth as Speedy pulled out a six-carat diamond engagement ring.

"Chantel. Will you—?" was all Speedy was able to get out before she yelled.

"Yes! Yes!"

Fuzzy shouted and jumped out of her seat into Speedy's arms. Everyone in attendance stood to their feet and clapped their hands for the two newlyweds.

"Thank you, baby."

"For what?" Speedy asked, while staring into her eyes.

"For making me the happiest woman on earth!"

Speedy loved to make Fuzzy smile, and every chance he got that's exactly what he did, and right now was no different.

"You think you're happy now, wait until later on tonight when I give you the big gift," he replied slyly while looking down at his crotch.

"I can't wait," Fuzzy replied, thinking about the amazing love they made before she went off to work.

Before she could lean in and get another kiss, Menace appeared out of nowhere and cleared his throat, startling both of them.

"Can I borrow your fiancé for a minute?" he asked Fuzzy as he kissed her on the cheek.

Over the past months, they had become very close and grew a brother-sister bond.

"Don't make me come looking for y'all," Fuzzy

joked before she walked away to entertain a couple of friends who showed up for the occasion.

Once she was out of earshot, Menace began.

"Yo! We need to meet up at the spot so Shelia can cook up about four of them things, because my phone has been ringing off the hook for the past couple of hours," Menace informed, hating to be away from the scene for so long.

Ever since they had started making real money, that's all he wanted to do.

"That's what's up. Give me about an hour. I gotta make a stop on the north side to pick up some change, and then I'll go by the stash house to get the work. Then I'll meet you at the spot."

After agreeing, they both went back to the get-together.

"Hey, baby. I got a few runs to make," Speedy informed Fuzzy as he slid into his motorcycle jacket.

As bad as Fuzzy wanted him to stay, she knew he had business to tend to, so she nodded her head in understanding and walked him to the entrance of the restaurant.

"Be safe out there, baby," she warned as she stood in front of him and zipped up his jacket.

"Ain't I always?" Speedy replied, before brushing a loose strand of hair out of her face.

Fuzzy grabbed his hands, closed her eyes, and placed them to her lips. "I love you," she whispered as she looked into his eyes.

Speedy matched her stare and looked deep into her soul before he replied. "I love you more!" he promised, and then he kissed her lips and walked out the door.

A cold chill ran down Fuzzy's arms when she heard the sound of his motorcycle start up. She made a silent prayer to the Man above that he make it back to her in one piece, before she turned around and walked back to the party.

15

When Speedy finished making his run on the north side, he headed to the stash house. He was sitting at the light when he noticed in his side mirror that the same black Crown Vic had been following him since he left Big Mama's Kitchen. When the light turned green, Speedy made a right turn, followed by another right, and then two more. After ending up at the same light as before, his suspicions were confirmed. He stared at the car that sat two cars behind him, and then dumped the clutch and fled through traffic. He glanced in his side mirror and watched as the Crown Vic dipped and dodged through traffic before running the red light in pursuit. The driver of the Crown Vic was more experienced than Speedy had anticipated, because within seconds, he was right on his tail.

"Oh shit!" Speedy screamed as the front bumper of the Crown Vic tapped his back tire, sending him fishtailing into the side of two parked cars before crashing into the back of an SUV.

Speedy was sent airborne over the sidewalk and landed on the front steps of an apartment building. The driver of the Crown Vic slammed on his brakes and brought it to a halt. Speedy heard the car door open, followed by a set of footsteps headed in his direction. He tried to reach for his gun, but he couldn't move his arm. He felt like a sitting duck, because he couldn't move either of his legs as well. Shock began to fill his body. He lay on his back staring into the sky through the shield of his helmet as the driver's shadow hovered over him. Speedy finally closed his eyes after seeing the nickel-plated revolver pointed down at his face.

"Who's out there?" an elderly lady shouted out while trying to open her door.

Before the driver was able to pull the trigger, the elderly lady opened her door and adjusted her glasses. The driver faded pack into the shadows unnoticed, hopped in his car, and peeled off down the block.

Once she saw Speedy lying on her front doorstep, she immediately made her way back into the apartment and dialed 911. The ambulance arrived within fifteen minutes to take Speedy to the emergency room while he hung on for dear life.

* * *

"How is he?" Fuzzy asked as she rushed into the waiting room where Menace and the crew were sitting.

Menace wouldn't allow anyone to go up to Speedy's room until she showed up.

"All the nurses and doctors told us was that he made it out of surgery," Menace informed. "The rest is up to him now."

Fuzzy stood there with a concerned look on her face for a minute before Menace spoke up again.

"Come on, Fuzzy. You know he's gonna pull through," he assured. "If he don't, I'ma personally kill him myself, bring him back again, and then let you kill him."

Fuzzy smiled lightly as she leaned into Menace's arm for support.

"You can bet your last dollar whoever is responsible for this shit is gonna pay," he whispered so no one could hear him but her.

There was no doubt in Menace's mind, or anyone else's in the crew, that someone was behind Speedy's accident, because there was no way he wrecked his bike on his own. Fuzzy took a step back and looked around into the faces of Speedy's mini army that sat around waiting to be given the word to set out revenge on the culprit. But as they all knew, Speedy had a long line of enemies, so figuring out which one it was would be the toughest task of all. Menace knew there was really only one person who had the money, the balls, and the manpower to set out to do such an act, but before he made his move, he wanted to hear his partner's side of the story.

"You ready to go up to his room?"

Fuzzy nodded and then wrapped her arms into his as he led the way to the elevator.

When they walked into Speedy's room, Fuzzy immediately broke down in tears. Just the sight of seeing the love of her life wrapped up like a mummy, with tubes coming out of every part of his body, was too much for her heart to bear.

"I still look good," Speedy joked in a low and strained voice.

Fuzzy's eyes lit up with joy from hearing him speak.

"Yes, you do, baby," she replied with a half-smile on her face as she walked over to his bedside.

It amazed her that no matter his situation, Speedy always made the best of it.

"I thought you left us, for a minute," Fuzzy admitted as she picked up his right hand and placed it on her stomach.

Speedy faintly smiled when he felt the baby kick at his hand.

"How is he?" Crystal asked as she walked up to Menace and gave him a hug followed by a kiss.

"All we know at this point is that he has a broken left arm, a couple of cracked ribs, and a slight concussion. We'll know more tomorrow when they run more tests on him."

Crystal nodded her head in understanding as

Tawana entered the room.

"I guess all we can do now is pray for the best," he finished as he stared into Tawana's eyes.

"Is everything okay?" Fuzzy asked as she watched a tear stream down the side of Speedy's face.

"Yeah, I'm good," he replied.

Fuzzy followed his eyes and noticed someone else had entered the room with Menace's friend. She didn't want to mention it at the time, but one of the females looked very familiar to her. She just couldn't put a finger on it at the moment.

"Will y'all excuse us for a minute?" Speedy asked, with his eyes locked on Tawana.

"I'll be outside in the waiting area," Fuzzy replied before giving Speedy a kiss on the lips and then walking out the door.

Tawana made her way over to Speedy's bed once Menace and Crystal made their exit. The only thing that could be heard was the beating of their hearts and the heavy teardrops hitting the floor.

"I'm so sorry," Tawana apologized before

taking his hand in hers. "I would've gotten here sooner, but you know."

Tawana looked down at her stomach and then back at Speedy. For the first time, Speedy noticed she wasn't pregnant anymore.

"The baby," he whispered in a barely audible voice.

A look of worry consumed his face.

"No, crazy! The baby's fine," she responded with a smile on her face, just thinking about her baby boy.

Her smile slowly faded and was replaced by the guilt of not telling Speedy she had the baby two weeks ago. She wanted to wait two more week so she could have a blood test to be sure if he was the baby's father or not.

"Why didn't you tell me?"

After explaining her reasons, Speedy understood. He tried to fight the feelings he still had for Tawana, but he knew he was fighting a losing battle within himself, and it showed in the tears that came out of his eyes. Silence filled the space between them before Speedy filled it with his big question. "So, who's the other possibility?"

Tawana wasn't expecting for him to ask that question, even though she had already gone over the answer 1,001 times in her head.

"King!" she answered honestly as she waited for Speedy to respond.

"Get the fuck out!" he demanded, snatching his hand from hers.

He felt as if his heart had just been ripped out of his chest. Out of all the people in the world, she chose to give herself to the only man who he hated with a passion.

"Now!" he screamed, causing Tawana to jump slightly.

"Please don't do this, Marcus," she begged, trying to put his hand back into hers.

"Don't touch me, bitch!" Speedy hissed, and snatched his hand back once more.

"Let me—!"

"Let you, what? Explain! There is no explaining this shit. I never want to see you again. To me, you're dead, bitch," Speedy cursed and slammed his fist on the bed.

"So, it's like that now?" Tawana asked. "We'll see if your little princess will be by your side when she finds out you never will walk again!"

Speedy strained his neck and looked into Tawana's eyes.

"Oh, you didn't know?" she asked after seeing the surprised look on his face.

She immediately regretted being the one to tell him the bad news, but it was too late.

"You lying bitch!"

Speedy didn't want to believe her, but the explanation she gave let him know she was telling him the truth.

"How do you think me and Crystal got back here? I had to lie to the fucking nurse out there and tell her I was your wife. After that, she told me everything I wanted to know, including that you may never walk again."

The news hit Speedy like a ton of bricks.

"She'll never be there for you the way I was.

Can't you see? The only reason the bitch is probably with you is because of your money," Tawana fumed, which only added fuel to the fire.

"Get the fuck out!" Speedy ordered again.

Tawana shook her head before heading toward the door.

"Oh yeah! Tell your baby daddy that he's dead. As soon as I get out of here, he's dead."

Tawana turned around, saw the fire in his eyes, and knew he wasn't just talking.

"Speedy, I know you don't think King had anything to do with this. To be mad with me is one thing, but to try and kill King for something he had nothing to do with is crazy."

Speedy's mind was made up and Tawana knew it. She just hoped he would have a change of heart by the time he was released. Tawana then headed out of the room with tears in her eyes and fear in her heart, before slamming the door behind her.

Fuzzy lay in the recliner beside Speedy's bed every night and fell asleep. Unbeknownst to her, Speedy was wide awake, with his eyes closed in a deep meditation about the argument that Tawana and he had the other day. When he opened his eyes, he watched Fuzzy as she bundled up under her coat. That was the first time Speedy ever doubted her love for him and looked at her in a different light. He wondered what her motive really was for being with him. He then closed his eyes and let the meds take over his mind, body, and soul before drifting off into a deep sleep.

16

While Speedy was recovering in the hospital, Fuzzy and Menace were in charge of handling his successful drug organization. As much as she hated to get herself involved in the lucrative game, she felt as if she had no other choice if she wanted to make sure Speedy secured his spot close to the top. The only person standing between Speedy and the number one position was the notorious King. Fuzzy vowed to herself to make sure Speedy reigned at the top before it was all said and done, by any means necessary.

After six long months of rehab, Speedy was able to recover and return back to the comforts of his own home. Even though he wasn't at 100 percent, just being able to come and go as he pleased was enough for him, at least for the time being.

"Hey, baby," Fuzzy called out from the foyer as she walked into the house and made her way to the bedroom, where she found him watching television.

"Hey, you," he replied as he turned his attention to Fuzzy walking into the room.

She let out a sigh of relief, kicked off her shoes, unbuttoned her blouse, and then walked over and stood in front of him.

"Can you unzip my dress," she asked.

Speedy happily obliged her as he watched her dress fall to the floor. At eight months pregnant, Fuzzy was still a sight to see. She carried the baby more in her ass and hips than her stomach.

"Can you wash my back?" Fuzzy whined as she made her way to the bathroom.

Speedy watched her backside all the way until she disappeared around the corner. When he was done, he helped her out of the Jacuzzi and back into their bedroom, where he lotioned her down from head to toe.

"Can I ask you a question, baby?"

"Of course, you can," Speedy replied as he walked over to the dresser and set down the bottle of lotion. "What's up?"

Fuzzy watched as Speedy made his way back over to the bed and took a seat by her side. She sat quiet for a minute, trying to figure out the right words to say before speaking. "When are you going to get back into the groove of things?"

"Why you ask me that? Did Menace mess up some money or drugs?" Speedy asked, jumping the gun.

"No! No!" Fuzzy assured him. "It's just," Fuzzy stuttered before wiping her sweaty hands against the bed to dry them.

Speedy looked at the nervous expression on her face.

"It's just what?" he questioned with wonder as the accusations that Tawana made at the hospital popped in his head. "Let me guess. You concerned about the money?"

Fuzzy couldn't believe the words that came out of Speedy's mouth. For as long as they had been together, not once had she asked him for a dime. Truth be told, she was the reason he was in the position he was in now.

"What?" Fuzzy blurted out in disbelief.

She stood to her feet and looked Speedy in his eyes. The stare-down lasted only a few seconds, but the tension in the room made it seem like hours.

"Just as I thought," Speedy replied, before walking out of the bedroom to get some fresh air.

Thirty minutes later Fuzzy walked outside to the backyard to join Speedy. She wanted to give the situation enough time to blow over before either of them made the vital mistake of saying something they would regret in the future. Fuzzy made her way up behind Speedy and hugged him tightly.

"I'm sorry, baby," Speedy apologized as he closed his eyes and inhaled her scent. "I have a lot of things on my mind right now."

Fuzzy let out a deep sigh before kissing the top of his head. She felt more comfortable talking with him when he was in a relaxed state of mind.

"You know I'm always here for you if you need me, right?' she asked, before she walked around in front of him.

"I know," he replied. "I can't believe I let that

bitch get into my head with all the bullshit about you being here because I was making money, and that you would leave if I was never able to walk again."

Fuzzy looked at him with a confused look on her face.

"What bitch?" Fuzzy asked, dumbfounded.

"Tawana," Speedy answered. "The day she came to the hospital, she told me all types of dumb shit. That's why I've been acting kind of distant since I was released," he admitted.

"Baby, I'll never leave you, especially when you're down," she promised. "I'm here for you in sickness and health, whether you're rich or poor and for better or worse." She kissed his lips after each promise. "And my favorite one: 'til death do us part. In other words, you're stuck with me forever." Fuzzy took a step closer to him. "Ain't no way you're getting this back," she laughed as she held up her wedding ring to his face.

The flood lights reflected off of the ring, sending a blinding sparkle into Speedy's eyes.

"You ready?" Fuzzy asked, grabbing him by his

hand.

"Where are we going?" Speedy asked while following behind her.

"We're going to the room for some makeup sex!" Fuzzy replied before turning around, dropping her robe to her feet, and then backing into the house.

Speedy had other plans in mind. He laid her on the living room floor and made love to her all through the night.

17

For the next few weeks, Speedy and his crew searched high and low for King, but he was nowhere to be found. It was damn near impossible for them to get the drop on him now, since he had beefed up his security since their run-in at The King's Palace. Other than that, things had been going just as Speedy had planned. He and Fuzzy's relationship was back to normal, he was back on his grind, and money was coming in faster than they could count it. Everything was cool until he received a phone call from Crystal.

"Speedy! Come to the hospital right now! Menace just got shot outside of our apartment door," she cried into the phone while trying to break down what she heard before the gunshot went off.

By the time Speedy and the crew reached the hospital, Crystal was at the entrance of the emergency room waiting. Before heading up to

Menace's room, Speedy ordered half of the crew to patrol the lobby area while the others stood outside of his room. He wanted to make sure Menace had eyes watching his back twenty-four hours a day.

A couple of days passed by, and Speedy stayed by his partner's side. The only time he left was to make a drop-off or pickup, or to take Fuzzy something to eat. That's if he didn't have one of the crew members do it for him.

"Don't you got better things to do?" Menace asked with his eyes still closed.

That was the first time Menace had spoken a word since he had been in the hospital. Speedy sat up in his chair and looked around at Crystal. He wanted to see if she also heard the voice, just to make sure he wasn't tripping.

"What? Y'all thought I could be taken out so easily? It's gonna take more than a fucking bullet to lay this old dawg down," Menace joked, followed by a light cough before continuing. "Besides, what would y'all do without me here?"

Speedy smiled and shook his head, happy that

his partner had come around. Crystal stood up from her pallet she had made on the window seat, and then she made her way over to his bed.

"Hey, baby," she spoke in a soft whisper. "How are you feeling?"

Crystal placed her hand on the side of Menace's face, leaned over his bed, and then kissed his dry lips.

"Besides this banging-ass headache, I'm good," he replied, squinting his eyes in an attempt to control the pain.

"Yo, did you see who did this to you?" Speedy interrupted, ready to send the crew out to handle business.

Menace's eyes turned cold and his lips began to shiver as he turned his head toward his partner before he spoke. "Yo, you wouldn't believe me if I told you," Menace assured him, before he gritted his teeth.

The thought alone made Menace so upset that his entire body began to tremble. "It was that bitch-ass nigga," Menace ranted, before his eyes started to roll to the back of his head and his tremble turned into a full-fledged convulsion.

"Oh my God! Menace! Menace!" Crystal called out as she shook him to bring him to, before taking off toward the door to get some help.

Speedy rushed to his partner and began to talk to him.

"Who was it?" Speedy questioned. "Come on, dawg! Don't do this right now."

The beeping from the machine was getting weaker. The machine flatlined just as the doctor and nurses ran into the room.

"Excuse me, but you all will need to step outside," the doctor ordered as he rushed to Menace's bedside.

Speedy and Crystal were ushered out of the room while the nurses hooked up the EKG to Menace's chest in an attempt to revive him. By the time Speedy and Crystal made it back to the waiting room with the rest of the crew, Speedy had made up his mind about who he thought the assailant was.

"I'ma get that nigger for you, Menace!" he

promised himself, before instructing the crew to meet back at the spot in an hour.

"Hit me up as soon as the doctor comes back and lets you know the deal," Speedy demanded before reaching in his pocket and pulling out a knot of money.

"I'm good," Crystal held up her hand and declined. "Just get whoever is responsible for doing this to my baby."

No words needed to be spoken between the two. Crystal knew the codes better than anyone else— things that are understood are never spoken. Crystal reached up and wiped away the tears from Speedy's eyes before he turned and walked out of the hospital.

* * *

As soon as Speedy pulled up to the spot, Crystal called his cell and informed him that Menace had slipped into a coma. Anger filled Speedy's soul as tears fell from his eyes. What really pushed him over the edge was when Crystal told him that if Menace did come out of his current state, he probably would be a vegetable for the rest of his life.

For seven straight days and seven straight nights, Speedy and the crew went on a bloody rampage and shot up every spot King owned on the north side, including his club. Anyone associated with him felt their wrath. The murder rate had reached an all-time high in Wilson during that period, and Speedy and his crew refused to let up the pressure until King came out of hiding. Speedy also lost a few soldiers in the war, and the only thing that ceased the death toll between the crew was when Speedy received a call from Lil Man.

"Big Homie, you're not gonna believe what just pulled out of Family Car Wash in front of me," he yelled into the receiver excitedly.

"What?" Speedy asked, still half sleep.

He glanced over at the night stand and saw that it was 9:30 in the morning.

"This better be good," he warned as he sat up in bed.

"Like I was saying," Lil Man continued. "Lucky and I were riding down Pender Street on our way to the school yard when the dude's candy-apple-red

Bentley GT pulled out in front of us."

Lil Man had Speedy's undivided attention. He snatched off the comforter from on top of him, which woke Fuzzy from her sleep.

"What's wrong, baby?" she questioned as she sat up behind him and placed her hand on his back.

Speedy raised his hand in the air, silencing her so he could finish hearing what Lil Man had to say.

"Take him out," Speedy ordered when Lil man was through talking. "Call me when it's done."

Speedy ended the call and then lay on his back after calling the hit. He watched the ceiling fan go round and round, and waited for Fuzzy to begin with the twenty-one questions he knew she was about to ask. He just knew she was about to try to talk him out of it, but she didn't.

"Damn!" Speedy moaned, when he felt the moistness from her lips kissing on his stomach. "Right there," he coached, once she put him in her mouth and looked into his eyes. Thirty minutes later, he was sleeping like a baby.

Speedy was awakened from his peaceful

slumber by the smell of cheese eggs, pancakes, and sausage. He glanced over at the clock. It read 12:10 p.m. He put both feet on the floor, stood to his feet, and grabbed the remote before turning on the television. That was something he did every morning before going into the bathroom to wash his face and brush his teeth. He always listened to the news before heading out into the world of the unknown.

"Hello, everybody. This is Zhaliah Thompson reporting live from the corner of Highway 264 and Forest Hills Road in Wilson."

The reporter turned, pointed, and continued, "You can see if you look behind me to my right that the police are directing vehicles and trying to gain control of the traffic that seems to be backed up for at least a mile or so. If you look to my left, you can see this was caused by a red Bentley GT that T-boned into the side of this Walmart eighteen-wheeler."

Speedy rushed back into the bedroom just as Fuzzy re-entered the room with a tray full of breakfast. Both stared wide-eyed at the television as they listened to the details.

"Witnesses say the driver of the red coupe was being chased by another vehicle. When the Bentley hit the eighteen-wheeler, the driver and passenger of the other vehicle got out and unloaded several rounds into each side of it. The names of the victims aren't being released at this time. What I can tell you though is the three occupants inside the Bentley GT are dead, including a small infant who couldn't have been more than a month or two. When will all the violence stop, people?" the reporter asked with sorrow in her voice. "This is Zhaliah Thompson signing out for WCLS Channel 11 News."

Before Speedy could make it back to the bathroom to spit out his toothpaste, his cell phone began to ring. He already knew what the call was pertaining to, so he answered without looking at the display screen.

"Speak," he angrily shouted into the phone.

There was a long silence before the caller responded.

"What!" he screamed, not believing his ears.

Fuzzy ran to the bathroom door and saw Speedy pacing back and forth in the middle of the floor.

"Meet me at the spot now!" he demanded, right before ending the call.

"What's the matter?" Fuzzy asked as Speedy stormed by her.

"We got a problem," Speedy informed her.

"Lil Man and Lucky said they're not the ones that completed the hit."

"What are you saying?"

"I'm saying we got a problem, because if they didn't do it, then who did?"

After Lil Man told him some old-model police-looking car had cut them off, they had lost the tail on King. Speedy began to wonder what the killer's motive was. Had they taken King out to take over his position at the top? So many questions ran through his head as he put on his clothes.

"I'll be back," Speedy assured Fuzzy, before grabbing his coat and keys and then heading to the spot to meet up with Lil Man and lucky to figure out their next move.

He was sure King's goons would seek revenge, so he wanted to be prepared.

* * *

Speedy sat outside the Wilson Chapel Church in his Lexus coupe as they carried the caskets out to the hearse. He felt all eyes would be on him if he decided to walk into the church to show his respect. Besides, he knew he wasn't welcome. Crystal now hated Speedy. Even though she wasn't sure, she had a feeling he was somehow involved with the death of her only sister and nephew. She made it very clear she didn't want anything from him. She even threw the money back in his face when he offered to finance the entire funeral.

After following the long line of mourners and spectators to the gravesite, Speedy still didn't bother to show his face and sat confined behind his dark tints. He watched each casket get lowered into the ground and said a silent prayer each time.

"I'm sorry," he whispered as he poured a shot of Henny down his throat.

After two more shots, Speedy wiped his eyes,

took one more look at the graves, and then pulled off down Lane Street. He then sat at the stop sign at the intersection of Park Avenue and Kenan Street, staring down the block of Park in deep thought about the events that had occurred over the past nine months of his life. The murders in which he was involved, the attempt on his own life, Tawana's betrayal, and his best friend lying in the hospital fighting for his life all weighed heavily on Speedy's conscience. No matter which way he looked at the situation, the bad outweighed the good.

Was it worth it? he thought to himself.

He then thought of his fiancée and the unborn child in her stomach.

"Go, nigga," the driver of the van behind him yelled out as he lay on his horn, snapping Speedy out of his thoughts.

Speedy looked left and then right as the strangest feeling came over him. He looked straight ahead, when it finally hit him. He cursed himself when he noticed that the driver across from him was wearing a ski mask over his face, as were the other occupants of the vehicles to his left and right. Before he could even put his foot on the accelerator to speed through the intersection, a van approached his driver's side and the side door slid open.

"You can make it hard or you can make it easy" were the only two options the masked man offered before jumping out with his gun drawn.

Before Speedy had the chance to respond, he was struck across his head and everything went black.

* * *

"Wake the fuck up!" Speedy heard a voice yell out from beside him, before he was punched in his face.

The darkness in the spacious room, along with the swelling of his eyes, made it hard for him to see who walked around in front of him.

"Nice of you to join us," the voice spoke again.

From the stale smell of tobacco lingering in the air, Speedy knew he was in an old tobacco warehouse. He just didn't know which one.

"You fuckin' pig," Speedy blurted out as he

coughed up a mouth full of phlegm and spat in his captor's face once his vision became clear.

He never would have guessed in a hundred years that he would be taken out by a cop.

"I wish my partner Russo was here to witness this shit," Detective Branch mumbled, while wiping the spit from his face.

Detective Branch was nothing like his partner. He was a short, black, potbellied, beady-eyed middle-aged man with a receding hair line. He vowed to Russo's daughters to take down the killers no matter what circumstances he would have to go through. Branch pulled out his service pistol and screwed a silencer onto the barrel of it. Just when he was about to pull back on the trigger, the sound of wheels rolling in their direction made him stall for a minute.

"I thought you were going to be a no-show," Branch speculated as the driver of the wheelchair pulled up beside him.

"You're supposed to be dead," Speedy said in disbelief as he looked into G Money's eyes.

"I know, right? I must admit. I look good for a dead man, huh?" G Money looked at Detective Branch and laughed.

"Awwww! Look at this nigga, Detective. He got the same look on his face Menace had before I put a hot one in him too."

Speedy couldn't believe what G Money had just admitted to doing. Guilt plagued his soul when he thought about the hit he put out that took the life of Tawana and her baby.

"So you're the one who shot Menace? I should've known something wasn't right when he told me I wouldn't believe who the shooter was."

G Money proudly nodded his head up and down while holding Speedy's gaze.

"Guilty as charged, and if it wasn't for that bitch of his turning on the porch light, I would've taken out his ass all the way," G Money promised. "I heard he's still in a coma. Too bad you won't meet the same fate as your friend," he threatened as he then held out his hand and gestured for Detective Branch to hand him the pistol.

Detective Branch smiled and cocked back the hammer before putting a bullet into the side of G Money's head. Speedy watched as blood and brain matter oozed out of the huge hole in the side of his head. Detective Branch then turned to finish the job he had started.

"You may have gotten away from me the first time I tried to take you out, but you won't this time," Branch promised as he pointed the gun in Speedy's face.

"I gotta admit, you sure do know how to ride the fuck out of a motorcycle. That little move you did by running through the red light really was impressive."

Detective Branch circled Speedy before stopping back in front of him.

"I guess the little old elderly lady can't save you now," he laughed before planting the barrel against the side of Speedy's head. "What the fuck!" Branch shouted when he heard several bullets whiz by him before landing in the crooked cops who guarded the entranceway of the door through which they had brought Speedy.

Branch tried to look through the darkness to see out where the shots had come from, but he couldn't pinpoint the area. Before being blinded by four red beams of light, Branch noticed a figure appear from the dark.

"Slim?" he questioned, wishing the image was an illusion.

Totally ignoring the question, Slim addressed the frightened detective.

"I wouldn't pull that trigger if I was you," he warned in a calm but sinister tone.

"Who? What are you doing here?" Slim smiled wickedly before answering. "I told you somebody had to pay for my brother's death."

"I-I-I had nothing to do with that! I told you that. It was all Russo's fault, man. He killed your broth—!" Branch tried to say.

"Shut your fat ass up! Russo's dead now, so his debt rolled over to you," Slim claimed.

Branch damn near jumped out of his skin as Slim's voice echoed through the room.

"Untie my nephew," he commanded Detective Branch.

After dropping his gun to the ground, Branch did as he was ordered.

"Get out of here, nephew. I got some unfinished business to tend to."

Speedy stood to his feet and looked at Detective Branch for one last time before drawing back and landing a backhand slap to the side of his face, knocking him off his feet.

"That was for Menace," Speedy told him as he watched Branch pick himself up off the ground. "See you in hell, muthafucka."

Speedy turned on his heels and limped out the door. Before he could make his exit, Speedy heard several footsteps running in the direction from which he had just come, before Detective Branch let out a deafening scream. When Speedy closed the door to the warehouse, he heard two gun shots ring out. As soon as he reached the corner, he heard a voice call out to him.

"You need a ride?" Fuzzy asked once she rolled

down the passenger side window.

Speedy forced a smile through his broken jaw and then got into the car.

"I still look good," he joked as he then leaned over and gave her a kiss on the lips.

His sense of humor never ceases to amaze me, she thought to herself as she pulled off into the night.

TO BE CONTINUED!

Text Good2Go at 31996 to receive new release updates via text message

BOOKS BY GOOD2GO AUTHORS

GOOD 2 GO FILMS PRESENTS

WRONG PLACE WRONG TIME WEB SERIES

NOW AVAILABLE ON
GOOD2GOFILMS.COM & YOUTUBE
SUBSCRIBE TO THE CHANNEL

THE HAND I WAS DEALT WEB SERIES
NOW AVAILABLE ON YOUTUBE!

THE HAND I WAS DEALT SEASON TWO
NOW AVAILABLE ON YOUTUBE!

THE HACKMAN
NOW AVAILABLE ON YOUTUBE!

To order books, please fill out the order form below:

To order films please go to *www.good2gofilms.com*

Name:_____

Address:_____

City: _____ State: _____ Zip Code: _____

Phone:_____

Email:_____

Method of Payment: Check   VISA   MASTERCARD

Credit Card#:_____

Name as it appears on card: _____

Signature: _____

Item Name	Price	Qty	Amount
48 Hours to Die – Silk White	$14.99		
A Hustler's Dream - Ernest Morris	$14.99		
A Hustler's Dream 2 - Ernest Morris	$14.99		
Bloody Mayhem Down South	$14.99		
Business Is Business – Silk White	$14.99		
Business Is Business 2 – Silk White	$14.99		
Business Is Business 3 – Silk White	$14.99		
Childhood Sweethearts – Jacob Spears	$14.99		
Childhood Sweethearts 2 – Jacob Spears	$14.99		
Childhood Sweethearts 3 - Jacob Spears	$14.99		
Childhood Sweethearts 4 - Jacob Spears	$14.99		
Connected To The Plug – Dwan Marquis Williams	$14.99		
Flipping Numbers – Ernest Morris	$14.99		
Flipping Numbers 2 – Ernest Morris	$14.99		
He Loves Me, He Loves You Not - Mychea	$14.99		
He Loves Me, He Loves You Not 2 - Mychea	$14.99		
He Loves Me, He Loves You Not 3 - Mychea	$14.99		
He Loves Me, He Loves You Not 4 – Mychea	$14.99		
He Loves Me, He Loves You Not 5 – Mychea	$14.99		
Lord of My Land – Jay Morrison	$14.99		
Lost and Turned Out – Ernest Morris	$14.99		
Married To Da Streets – Silk White	$14.99		
M.E.R.C. - Make Every Rep Count Health and Fitness	$14.99		
My Besties – Asia Hill	$14.99		
My Besties 2 – Asia Hill	$14.99		
My Besties 3 – Asia Hill	$14.99		
My Besties 4 – Asia Hill	$14.99		
My Boyfriend's Wife - Mychea	$14.99		
My Boyfriend's Wife 2 – Mychea	$14.99		
Naughty Housewives – Ernest Morris	$14.99		
Naughty Housewives 2 – Ernest Morris	$14.99		
Naughty Housewives 3 – Ernest Morris	$14.99		

Naughty Housewives 4 – Ernest Morris	$14.99		
Never Be The Same – Silk White	$14.99		
Stranded – Silk White	$14.99		
Slumped – Jason Brent	$14.99		
Supreme & Justice – Ernest Morris	$14.99		
Tears of a Hustler - Silk White	$14.99		
Tears of a Hustler 2 - Silk White	$14.99		
Tears of a Hustler 3 - Silk White	$14.99		
Tears of a Hustler 4- Silk White	$14.99		
Tears of a Hustler 5 – Silk White	$14.99		
Tears of a Hustler 6 – Silk White	$14.99		
The Panty Ripper - Reality Way	$14.99		
The Panty Ripper 3 – Reality Way	$14.99		
The Solution – Jay Morrison	$14.99		
The Teflon Queen – Silk White	$14.99		
The Teflon Queen 2 – Silk White	$14.99		
The Teflon Queen 3 – Silk White	$14.99		
The Teflon Queen 4 – Silk White	$14.99		
The Teflon Queen 5 – Silk White	$14.99		
The Teflon Queen 6 - Silk White	$14.99		
The Vacation – Silk White	$14.99		
Tied To A Boss - J.L. Rose	$14.99		
Tied To A Boss 2 - J.L. Rose	$14.99		
Tied To A Boss 3 - J.L. Rose	$14.99		
Tied To A Boss 4 - J.L. Rose	$14.99		
Time Is Money - Silk White	$14.99		
Two Mask One Heart – Jacob Spears and Trayvon Jackson	$14.99		
Two Mask One Heart 2 – Jacob Spears and Trayvon Jackson	$14.99		
Two Mask One Heart 3 – Jacob Spears and Trayvon Jackson	$14.99		
Wrong Place Wrong Time	$14.99		
Young Goonz – Reality Way	$14.99		
Subtotal:			
Tax:			
Shipping (Free) U.S. Media Mail:			
Total:			

Make Checks Payable To:
Good2Go Publishing
7311 W Glass Lane,
Laveen, AZ 85339

8/17

CPSIA information can be obtained
at www.ICGtesting.com
Printed in the USA
LVOW03s1456170717
541649LV00012B/1116/P

9 781943 686377